SUGAR SAND ROAD

Katie Schulze-Bahn

ISBN: 978-1-09836-388-8

CONTENTS

This book is dedicated to my children.
You are the loves of my life, and I've never met such
wonderful people as you. I am honored to be your mother.
I love you, I love you, I love you, I love you.
Sophie, Brody, Ellie, and Ty.
B.E.S.T.

I would like to thank:

My husband Dr. Paul A. Bahn, III

My wonderful parents Vince & Carol

My brother Steve Schulze

My [late] grandparents Louis and Erma

My two rescued hound dogs Penny & Ruby

My dear friend Crissy Dupery-Fingeroth

My dear friend Deb Eaton

My dear friends who are no longer with us: Denise Rago-Wallace, Frieda Heston, Gina "G" Zucker, Meg Blong, Narberth "Narby" Gotshall, and Shirley "Kran" McNeill

My Friend Frank Finale

My friend Joey Houlihan

My friend Linda Greenlaw

My cover artist Vanessa Altimari

Last but certainly not least: My entire team at BookBaby

"If you like a solid coming of age story,
then hold on to your hat.
You're going to like this kid."

- J.V. Houlihan: a columnist known as
The Block Island Ferry Scribbler, author, freelance writer,
and former middle and high school English teacher

"As a lifelong fisherman, I can attest
to this as a classic and salty read.
Job well done by my friend Kate."

- Linda Greenlaw: *NY Times* best-selling author,
world-renowned female fishing captain

"I've known Kate a long time.
Her wit and wild energy really shine through
in this classic romance for all ages."

- Frank Finale: beloved & award-winning
Jersey Shore author

PROLOGUE

For those of you who've not yet had the chance to enjoy Long Beach Island or The Pine Barrens – both in NJ – may this inspire you to do so.

They don't call it "The Garden State" for nothing.

Nota bene: although some people,
places and events in this novel are based
on some of my own true-life stories,
this is a book of complete fiction.

Chapter 1:

SALTY BEGINNINGS

My youngest years and memories come from a small island off the southern New Jersey coast. Only a few feet above sea level, eight miles long and a mile at its greatest width, it was a quaint one. Few trees dotted the sandy landscape, but greenery did abound in forms of lilacs, hydrangea, beach roses, and wild honeysuckle in the spring and summer. Scrub pines, low to the sandy earth, hugged the island in groups here and there year-round. Of course, there were the great dunes too: rippling in a green sea of their own, with tiny boardwalks passing through them, leading to the beautiful white sand beaches on the other side. Mostly crushed-shell streets, driveways, and paths were our means of transportation. Some homes were large: old sea captains' estates. Our home on the bay was modest, however: an old fisherman's cottage with faded cedar-shake siding and white shutters, attached to our little marina on the water and (even smaller) bait shop in the middle. The sunsets were breathtaking from our docks, but were not to be outdone by the scent of salt air always wafting in off the water. The sound of sailboat masts dinging in the wind from the metal rope loops was a familiar sound, and the gulls were like pets: always present and begging for a scrap of food in the form of minnows and other tiny fish when we'd cut up the bait. I continuously found it amusing when they battled over the diminutive fish, only to be let down when their finned snacks slipped between the chum-encrusted gaps in the dock, leaving the birds aghast, with elongated necks and cocked heads going side to side. Following their confusion, they always seemed to stare at me blankly as I laughed at the entire scene. It seemed only fair payback when they'd wake our family up at sunrise by dropping giant clams on the roof in efforts to crack them open to get at the meat inside: part breakfast, part revenge. I always woke up with a little giggle at our natural alarm clocks, but I knew my parents opened their eyes grumbling under their breath from a startle to their day. Truth be told, we needed to be up early to get the shop up and running anyway, and—deep down—I think we were all grateful to be part of a place so unique.

The islanders were hardy, almost gruff, but tight-knit. We had to be. Winters were long and gray, and lacked activity, unlike "in season" which ran from Memorial Day to Labor Day. That time was bustling with the rich out-of-town folks, who came with fancy cars and wine-filled weekend plans, gourmet dinner outings, and obnoxious, attention-seeking laughter. Unfortunately, we all had to bite our tongues. These people were the ones we relied on to make money in the summer, so we could make it through the off-season. We depended on each other to keep spirits up during those dreary winters, as we anticipated the warm and sunny days ahead, which would start the yearly cycle all over again. One bit of sunshine in my life was our family friend, Narby.

A few decades older than my folks, and about forty years my elder, Narby was a little thing standing barely five feet tall, full of feistiness, life, and lots of love. She lived in the apartment tucked snugly between the bait shop and our cottage. Narby had gotten to know my parents when they'd bought the property from her on a whim when they'd first married and helped them grow it into the small but thriving and well-known business it'd become. Though Narby's selling of the shop was an intended step toward retirement, she continued to offer advice, labor, and motherly care: like the love that held our sandy little shoal together. The shop and this way of life was hers since she had no family. She didn't sell it to my parents for any reason other than knowing they'd be in her life forever, and they'd let her stay a part of the shop, too, by living right on the property. Because my parents were often so busy running the business, and I had no siblings or cousins, aunts, or uncles, she sort of took me in as the young buddy that I was. She helped watch me as a baby-sitter of sorts after I was born, and—though not blood-related—was family; likewise, we were hers. I learned much about the ways of saltwater life from her, especially how to sail.

Narby had been sailing her whole life, and as her little apprentice, I was next in line to harnessing the wind. It was an easy task for her, because—I too—was taken with the peace of the breeze and gliding through the water without the sounds of an engine or the scent of diesel. Being underway meant harmony, fresh air, and being taken out to a place of wonder with nothing but the open ocean below. We didn't start small either. My "ease" into becoming first mate, started on her twenty-seven-footer. It was a simple, single hull, main and jib sailboat, but it took skill. It was beautiful with sleek white sails and polished teak deck. No joke for an eight-year-old (which I was at the time), but I took to it fast. I learned the ways of the ropes, the sails, the tiller, and my sea legs quickly became as sturdy as my land legs.

By the time I was ten, I'd had plenty of wins under my belt from the local yacht clubs. I wasn't the yachtie type, of course, but I was racing against the rich summer folks' kids. It wasn't a rarity that they stuck their children in all-day sailing schools… often against their spoiled offspring's wills. But for me—a child coming from a humble background—I felt fortunate enough just to be there and have access to different kinds of watercraft to develop my knowledge. The managers of the clubs were locals too, so that was my in. Narby knew them well and our fees were always waived; otherwise, I'd have not been able to afford it. Though I never did make a life-long friend in any of my fellow sailors, those days made me proud. I was different from them through and through: a cute little girl, with the personality of a tomboy. Yet,

I was their competition. Money didn't matter when it came to shear know-how. To hang around those kids and truly make friends, I'd have needed some refining though. But Narby accepted me for who I was. Sailing with her on *Piney Power* made me feel more alive than ever, and her stories kept me laughing. But there was one story that kept me more curious than anything: a farm on the mainland in this "land of the pines" that she'd inherited by generations of family. It's where her boat got the name.

Her stories of the place seemed organic, wild, and endless, but—mostly—enigmatic. I think she knew it kept me wondering, and Narby liked it this way. It was a sort of unspoken knowledge that we'd always have this *secret farm* to talk about, and never run out of conversation. The only connecting piece to this place, other than the name of the boat, was an old truck that had been left to her along with it. It was sky-blue, from the forties or fifties, with wooden panels above the sides of the bed. I loved riding in it to go pick up ice for the bait shop, run errands, or just take for rides on summer evenings to get ice cream on the other side of the island. Her stories aboard the boat and riding in the truck bonded us closely and, somehow, vicariously linked me to the farm, too. Though I'd never even seen a picture, I felt a connection to it.

Chapter 2:

THE DARK SIDE OF SUMMER

The storms on the island that would roll in from offshore came in late summer and early fall, and often brought the year-round community together even more tightly when they knocked the power out or flooded the streets. We'd be forced to kayak to each other's homes and grill the food that'd otherwise spoil in our fridges and freezers, making for impromptu "storm parties." It was almost as if we looked forward to the short stints of foul weather as an excuse to take a break from our hard work of seasonal island life. The gray clouds would roll in, making a grand entrance with far-off lightning whose partner of thunder would rumble the cedar shakes blanketing the homes, giving us warning of the approaching weather. The boats would rock, occasionally, knocking on the docks, and the seabirds would fly with a drunken style, caught in the ever-changing winds. But there was one storm that gave no warning.

In late August, just after my tenth birthday, it rolled in, and it rolled in quickly. But this massive front was to be very different. The wind picked up with no precursor of the normal strong breeze, like other storms, and the clouds came in black: like a giant vulture with wings reaching for miles across a dark foreboding sky. When the first blare of lightning hit, the rain was already coming down heavily. When storms like this came, we always had a pact to search each other out to make sure we were all accounted for, and then assess what work needed to be done to hunker down, but my parents were nowhere. As I searched the bait shop, Narby hurried in after me. At the same time, we stopped yelling for them, looked at each other with concern, and a rather ominous look came across her face. She spoke the words flatly remembering something, "They're on the water." They'd been gathering some other boats to bring in and tie up since it had been a slow and overcast day. My heart sank. I could feel something in my veins that gave me chills, and I knew they were in trouble. I ran out to the end of the main dock with Narby by my side. As we strained to see through the curtain of rain that came down all around us, we saw them. There they were, in a tiny red crabbing boat, bobbing helplessly in the middle of the bay. Without thinking, I hopped into another crabber, and began to pull the engine rope to start her up. Narby grabbed me right back out, and reminded me, "It's metal, Kate, get out!" As I jumped back onto the dock, we stood side by side, helpless.

Then we watched—as if in slow motion—a gigantic, gnarled hand of lightning came down from the black sky, spread out over what seemed to be the entire bay, and struck their tiny crabbing boat directly in the center with its longest and thickest finger. I knew at that moment, they were gone. I knew at that moment; my childhood would change forever.

Immediately after the tragedy, Narby took over the job of my parents: trying to keep our business up and running, all while trying to be my full-time guardian. But it was hard, as Narby often only had the one "volunteer job" of being my baby-sitter in the past. But now, taking on a business that she'd not fully run by herself for so many years—as well as trying to care for me around the clock—was just too much. She eventually put the shop up for sale after asking for my permission (contingent that it not transfer deed until the upcoming school year ended), and—though it meant uncertain change for the future—at least we found solace in each other, and the fact that I'd still be around familiar places and faces for the time being. Too much change at once would be bad. She wanted to put me, and only me, first. Whatever happened, we would make it through together.

School began solemnly for me that year. Kindergarten through third had been on the island, with just the local kids. But now entering fourth grade at a new school, I was bussed to the mainland just over the bridge to the adjacent bay town, with an entirely new group of kids added to the mix of my familiar island crew. Adjusting to the crowd, along with trying to move forward in agony with my loss from just a few weeks prior, was debilitating. Constantly walking around with a knot in my throat and a pit in my stomach, I felt as if at any time I might succumb to my self-pity. It was an empty hole filled with nothing but pain, which seemed like it would never fade or fill up again with joy. To make matters worse, I was so sad and detached, that kids avoided me. At a time when I could have used a friend, I was alone. Perhaps had they shown a little sympathy; the new kids would have realized I wasn't weird, or an outcast, after all. I was just hurting.

Although pretty, I was a bit of a wild and messy looking kid, of course, whose personality usually matched that. I was the perfect combination of my parents: with my mom's big greenish-blue eyes (that Narby often told me changed like the colors of the sea), and my dad's wild, sandy-colored hair: the saltier the air, the curlier it got. I guess it gave an appearance of being uninhibited and free: just like my character. Maybe that was off-putting to some. I was a good kid though: always standing up for others, with wit and feistiness that made me fearless. Always covered in some sort of sand and not really caring about my looks; the delicacy that one would expect to come from a girl so daintily constructed was all but lost when someone got to know me. Rubber boots or flip flops, t-shirts or hooded sweatshirts, and usually some form of jeans (whether full-length, or having been cut somewhere between the length of ankle or mid-thigh) was all I wore. But no matter what clothing I was covered with on the outside these days, on the inside I was bare to the bone, with a heart so vulnerable and exposed to the world.

If even there was an effort made as a welcome from anyone, I didn't see it. I was too far under in my own hurt, and my low-hanging head. But Narby reminded me day after day to "Stay strong, stay true to myself, and though I'm tough on the outside, my insides are still sweet… just like a coconut." But my sweetness felt bitter. The new kids—the masses of them—didn't understand my pain, and it showed. Even my old island pals had seemed to have given up on me, as if they just couldn't save me from my own misery. Eventually, they avoided me completely, and I was alone. I had no will to make friends, so at some point, I just gave up.

With only a few months left of the school year, Narby realized the depth of my depression. My eyes were sunken with sadness too deep to understand. It was an appearance of having been through a time of great loss far beyond what a child should suffer and pushing forward just to survive. It was hard on her to see me like this, and Narby knew it was time for a change, even with only a short time left for school to end.

She altered the contingency on the sale of the bait shop, and time seemed to be in our favor, as it sold within a few months and left us with an open-ended decision. With my consent once again—she decided then and there that we were moving, and not just moving, but moving to her mysterious farm in this place called *The Pine Barrens*….

Chapter 3:

GATEWAY TO THE PINES

The Pines Barrens of South Jersey span over one million acres. Some call them the "Pinelands" or simply the "Pines." They abound with flora and fauna unique to the area, like gems scattered everywhere, but hidden just the same. The sandy roads resemble fine sugar, running in all different directions, and often splitting off into trails leading to forgotten railroads, settlements, and ruins. Rivers and streams snake through the dense undergrowth like a never-ending labyrinth and are browned from the bog iron and cedar that color their endlessly trickling waters. Farms of this South Jersey forest are dispersed throughout the land: cranberry bogs and blueberry fields, orchards and sod, horses and cows. Days past were when it seemed more appreciated by the Native Americans and settlers who'd called it home, than the current days just seen from empty roads that cut through the woods like highways to nowhere. Essentially, to most who are local—and even more so, for those who are not—the place is unknown beyond tales or pictures, a vastness with lost and unfounded stories. To me, it was my new home.

The tiny town we were headed was surrounded by the forest, many farms, and had a downtown area with only a little brick school house with a baseball field, the post office, a church, a cemetery, a bar, the town hall, and a small grocery store with the bare necessities. I would have little time to explore it all right away as I'd be jumping right back into school again, but at least the season was warming up and there were plenty of months ahead for adventure once school ended. I didn't quite feel up to wandering yet anyway, nor was I in a happy enough place to do so, but I had hope deep down this place would help me. It might take a while, but I felt something good could come of it. It was my first glimmer of optimism, and I could smell positive change in the pine-laced air as we arrived.

Narby's farm was a good welcoming start. It was a virtuous place to be free, with open fields, orchards, and berry patches. Most had been overgrown since it had been left to her years ago, but I was sure once things settled, we could put our minds to fixing it up. These plans in my head kept the horrid memories of the tragedy to a minimum. The farmhouse itself was impressive. In a sense, it was reminiscent of the grand old sea captains' homes, with a big wrap-around porch and cedar shake shingles, although these shingles were painted white, and not worn from the sun to a faded gray as on island. The white picket fence at the front of the property's edge added the finishing touch and matched the house. Heirloom bulb flowers were beginning to pop up in beds around the porch, random sheds, barns, and other little dwellings around the property. Covered over by some vines and filled with weeds, the beds would need some love, but *it will keep me busy*, I thought hopefully. The daffodils had already sprung up with crocuses arbitrarily in the yard, but most lined the simple sand path that ran from the porch to a little picket gate under an arbor that sat in the center of the fence, and separated the entire farm from a sandy dirt road. I imagined that days gone by must have shown this place in all its splendor and I hoped we could bring it back to life just the same. The air was fresh: a mixture of pine needles and wood, flower blossoms, turned earth, cut grass, and spring rain, complete with the hum of bees coming out of their winter slumber in search of the season's first nectar. A cool breeze seemed to blow through the trees. It sounded so familiar, yet I couldn't quite place it. It gave me a little chill and a hopeful curiosity. Maybe this was a sign of good things to come.

For a kid of age ten, switching from a completely different environment and school at the end of fourth grade was a big change but maybe for the best. It kept my mind off the tragedy, and I wasn't surrounded by things that constantly reminded me of the loss of my only blood family. When we'd moved back to Narby's mainland mystery farm, winter had already passed, and the beginning of spring meant I'd be back to wearing flip flops, tee-shirts, and those cut-offs of some form in no time at all. Normally, I wore the jean-type bottoms, but my "fancy" chino shorts were embroidered with a plethora of nautical emblems: lobsters, fish, anchors, and so forth. Narby had picked these up for me from different sailing ports as treats to "dress me up a bit" for special occasions, as she knew dresses were completely out of the question to me. I suppose she thought I'd find a sense of style in time. (I thought style was ridiculous.) But I always said thank you and pretended to like them. To look halfway decent for my first day at the new school, I agreed to wear a pair. I went with the seagulls. Although trying to forget the island for the time being, they did offer a connection to memories of my parents, so I figured they were a lucky charm. I really was a pretty girl, and all Narby had hoped was to bring out the femininity in me a little more from time to time; make me a little spiffy, I supposed.

No sooner than putting on the shorts and walking into the new school, I realized very quickly that my attire was—as always—very different. When entering class on the first day (escorted by the principal for a feeling of security, kindness, and welcome), there was a deafening silence from the other classmates. Back to my original small-town island class size, it was half-filled with wealthy farm-owner's kids whose parents I would learn held the land of prestigious horse properties (I suppose equivalent in arrogance to the yachties back on island), and the other half with farmers' kids (those who actually took care of the farms). And I—well I—was somewhere in my own world, washed ashore from a little island, a fish out of water. I was a beach girl, surrounded by Polos and plaid shirts. The silence was only broken with a chuckle, let out anonymously somewhere in the small crowd. I later found out the snickering was led by the class bully: a popular girl named Kitty. Off the bat, she hated me. Right then and there, I had a gut feeling I was her new tear-down project. Her nastiness looked etched in her eyes, and if it weren't for my resilience that I'd learned too quickly for a kid of such a young age, she'd have eaten me alive right then and there. She was as sly and cunning as a cat on the prowl, probably complete with sharp retractable claws too. But she'd probably never experienced real pain or a life of honest-to-goodness work ethic either. She was privileged, and her primped appearance and snobby personality proved so. Me being the total opposite type of person she was, posed a new challenge for her. She didn't know how to deal with someone thick-skinned and unique, as she was probably accustomed to breaking people down very quickly to stake her claim as alpha female and convert them to her way and her way only. But at the time being, my skin was softer; worn thin from the recent events, and even *I* was vulnerable. I wondered how long I could keep her fooled. I figured this relocation to a new town, home, and school was my only hope of recovery. If someone took that optimism away from me, I wasn't sure how I'd ever move on.

The principal and teacher had sympathy for me (and probably saw right through Kitty's fake smiles anyway when she tried to win over the school staff), so they sat me next to a kind girl named Dorey who seemed humble and with little judgment. Although I'd later come to learn she was one of the wealthy ones who owned a horse farm, Dorey wasn't like those fancy girls who rode English style and competed at significant competitions. She was more of a country girl, and I liked her ruggedness. Over this, we bonded. It made for a more calmed feeling when I left for school day after day the rest of that school year.

I still seemed the target of the mean girl and her clique of snobs though. Relentlessly, they bullied me. They made fun of everything from my clothing to my tragedy. It seemed so inhumane. For a child to make fun of another's loss of their only family showed what a monster she really was. Money couldn't buy class, and this was living proof. Even her friends seemed taken aback by this new low to which she'd sunk just to hurt someone. But for fear of retaliation from their queen bee, they stayed silent. Dorey always had my back, but they shut her down just as quickly. Kitty and her posse had no remorse or kindness for anyone, especially anyone who challenged Kitty. I couldn't quite wrap my head around how cruel they could be, and it often made my stomach turn. At some point, my trying to fight for a fresh start and stand up to them, wore me down a bit. I never showed it on the outside, but I needed an escape before it surfaced, and they'd take notice. It really did bring back that pit feeling in my stomach. For this reason, I often asked to go to the nurse.

With the same sympathy that my teacher had given me the first day of school, she allowed me to go as often as needed to the nurse's office. I didn't take advantage of my teacher though with our little unspoken agreement to temporarily escape the bullies or the upset stomach: both of which quickly went away the moment I entered the nurse's office. I just went when it was unbearable, and this nurse seemed to help greatly. Her name was Mrs. Mills.

She was a kind-hearted, local woman with big curls of gray to her shoulders. She had glasses and would often tilt her head downwards to see over the top rim of them whenever someone spoke to her. It was almost a gesture of interest and humanity, to show someone she cared deeply, when she made that eye contact. She was downright sympathetic, just what I needed to pick me up when I felt low. She had this neat wooden duck collection, too; decoys I think they were. Ironically, she'd brought many of them from the marsh towns back near the island, as her family had vacationed there for many years. Her great-grandfather had been one of those sea captains, and she'd summered in one of those grand homes as a child. Not as one of the privileged upper-class

13

snobs of summer who'd mostly purchased them only to knock them down and build more modern, luxury homes, but simply as someone enjoying family history and keeping the traditions alive for other generations. I guess, just like Narby's connection to the Pines, Mrs. Mills had a connection to the island as well. It was ironic to have the salty link, and—although we didn't talk about it since she knew my recent history—it offered a comforting, immediate, and tacit bond. I really enjoyed visiting her. I guess she caught on to my plan of daily escapes and knew my stomach aches weren't as bad as they often were as school continued, but not once did she let on that my situation be less than it appeared. She always sat me down, took my temperature, and let me lay on the nurses table. As I lay there, we just chatted. I guess the whole scene would have been redolent of a therapist's office: patient on the chaise lounge, therapist taking notes and intrigued by thoughts coming from the one in need of help and direction. And she often gave that direction, too. Just like Narby told me to stay strong, she'd say, "This too shall pass."

Had it not been for Mrs. Mills and Dorey, the rest of the school year would have made me completely despondent. But I knew summer was coming, and although I'd not see Dorey much out of school since she'd have so much work to do on her parents farm, I'd finally have time to explore, and take on my new-found hope.

And that first bit of hope came in the form of a blond-haired boy.

Chapter 4:

HOPE

The end of school came quickly, and the first day of summer break began with a beautiful blue sky, and a warm, fresh, sweetly scented air. It was the perfect day for my first venture, and so I took the opportunity after my breakfast to go explore and walked off the property out front. Standing on the edge of the road, I had two options: going one way would lead into town, and the other would lead to the great pine forest. I chose the latter, of course. I shut the gate behind me and started walking off on my adventure. Narby had mentioned how safe the town was, so I felt comfortable enough to go out on my own.

The sandy road ran like a thick tree trunk through the woods, with scraggly branch-like trails stemming off it. It felt warm and familiar under my bare feet. I looked down as I walked to take in the resemblance of the feeling from back home, but when I looked up again, I noticed someone standing still up ahead.

The other child made the first move to come toward me. With a small bit of worry that this person would be another bully from school, instinct told me to run. But heartache—and possible desperation for a friend—made me stay put. As he neared, I felt a bit calmer that it was a farmer's kid (at least judging by his attire), and not one of the polo-privileged snobs, but I did not recognize his smiling face. Even in a small class size of maybe twenty in each grade and only two hundred or so in the entire school of grades K-8, he was unfamiliar. I was a kid that noticed everything and remembered everyone. If even someone passed by me in the hall once, I'd always remember their face, but I couldn't place him. He had light blond hair: a few uneven lengths poking out from under a big John Deere tractor hat, a little too big for his head. He was barefoot too, and his eyes gleamed blue from the sunlight sneaking in from the side of the hat rim in the late morning sun. He had on a short-sleeved, button-down, plaid shirt, tucked into a pair of jeans pulled up high at his waist, and complete with a plain, leather belt. A thumb tucked into one pocket, and in the other hand—a group of little white flowers that I caught a whiff of as he approached. They smelled sweet like the way candy tasted. For a moment, we were silent and just stared at each other, and then I smiled back. For the first time in almost a year, I felt more hope than ever.

His growing smile and words to follow instantly made me feel welcome. He was kind and unassuming when he spoke. Completely unassertive and clearly comfortable in his own skin. I was admirably intrigued.

"Hi!" he said a little too loudly but smiling even bigger.

A bit [but only a small bit] apprehensive by his volume, I replied shyly and smiled a little, "Hi."

"I know this road better than anyone," he said and seemed to puff his chest with pride at this explanation.

I replied, "It's nice and sandy. Looks like sugar."

His eyes lit up. "We call it *sugar sand* around here!"

Then, jumping from one topic to another, he pulled his other hand from his pocket, and held it out. "Want some? It's teaberry gum."

I'd never heard of it, but my interest made me respond quickly, "Sure."

I stuck out my hand and put it in my mouth. It tasted like a combination of winter-mint and cherry bubblegum.

"Teaberries are all over the ground, but you have to look underneath the leaves to see the berries," he pointed all around with no real direction.

Jumping back to my previous comment, and maybe trying to open up a bit about my tragedy in an ingenuous way without missing my chance to do so, I spoke solemnly, "It reminds me of the sand back home."

A little smile of comfort and reminiscence came over my face. A glimmer of optimism that I'd made a friend perhaps, whom I could trust not to hurt me when feeling so lost.

"Back home?" he inquired, trying to figure out where I came from and decipher the longing tone in which my voice had taken.

"I moved here a few months ago, from the island. The island was what I meant by home."

"The island?" he asked as his eyes lit up at this and his volume went beyond the initial greeting, and it seemed his lucky day. "Wow!"

I had a feeling of momentary celebrity and then continued.

"Well, I liked it there..." On this note my voice trailed off, and an unexpected frown came over my face as I turned my head and stared off into oblivion. I felt a little tear pressure from behind my eyes when the thought of my parents came into my mind. I didn't expect to feel this yearning for my family to sneak up and hit me in the chest so fast, but I thought perhaps this boy would be compassionate.

He must have noticed my discomfort and changed the subject so as to avoid making me suffer through an explanation. It seemed like perfect timing for a good transition, and he motioned for me to "come 'ere" with a loud whisper. It was funny how kids could jump so quickly from one emotion from the next, so openly and lax.

"Look," he whispered again, as his finger pointed off into the abyss of the woods.

I finally focused on a chipmunk, after trying to find its small, camouflaged self. He made the little creature seem larger than life just to make me happy. I smiled again, and he smiled right back intensely.

He motioned for me to follow, and I copied his hunched position as we snuck toward the chipmunk. As soon as I stepped on a branch, making a tiny cracking sound, the little animal scampered hurriedly away into a fallen, rotting log of a tree.

He turned to me to puff out a tiny laugh of air through his nose, "Humpf. Buggers! They're always too quick!" he declared.

We straightened our crouch of a stance and—out of nowhere—I quietly said, "I'm Katie. Most people call me Kate."

His smile grew, and he said, "I'm Will, and I like your name just the way it is, Katie." His eyes were so bright. Up close, I saw just how gentle and joyful this boy was, and I'd truly never seen eyes that happy.

Our eyes met and hung on a little more than an average introduction. He then quickly handed me the flowers he'd been holding, almost embarrassed; briefly breaking the moment between us. I swear, for a second, I saw him blush. The flowers were lily-of-the-valley, growing wildly in the woods, and he told me he picked them right before he found me. They smelled heavenly.

We began to wander off into the woods, chatting as aimlessly as the trails ran. It was comfortable, and I trusted him. Blindly, I trusted this person.

With a more serious tone this time, and the truth of wanting to know more about me, he asked directly, "What grade are ya in?"

"Going into fifth. How about you?" I replied.

"Fourth..." he said matter-of-factly, but open-endedly enough to let me know there was more to follow. So, I didn't speak.

"I know a girl named Dorey in your grade though. She's real nice," he concluded.

"I sat next to her this year! She sure is nice!" I finished.

He started again, almost a hint of shyness in his voice, "I don't really have a lot of friends, but I don't mind. I like it that way."

He spoke almost with a little bit of longing, perhaps feeling outcast like me. But at the same time, he meant what he said: he *didn't* mind. I believed him. He seemed content to be free of any clique and happy to entertain himself. He didn't need to explain. I understood exactly how he felt. I could already tell he was an old soul like me. He was wise beyond his years but trying to figure out where his confidence fit in with other kids more worried about popularity and the latest trends—those who were trying to stake their claim as the classroom bosses. He was above them, but their judgment was made to make him feel exiled and belittled. I was envious, as my confidence was all but gone nowadays. I had no friends either. But—here he was, still by my side, wandering the woods. I wanted to know about him just as much as he clearly did me.

"Where do you live?" I asked.

"Just down the road," he pointed back to where he'd come from. "My dad is the manager at a farm." His puffing pride returned.

"Wow, so he gets to work with animals all day?" I inquired excitedly.

"Oh, no. Sorry, I meant fruits and vegetables," he corrected me with a small giggle.

I couldn't quite wrap my head around it, but I wanted to stay by his side until the sun went down. I felt safe around this person. Despite having only just met, I felt protected in ways unexplainable.

Still wandering, we'd made it to a stream that flowed into a little shallow pool. It was my introduction to the dark water of the area, of which Narby had spoken in her many captivating tales. There was a mound of sticks off to one side of the faster moving part of the stream, seeming to trap the silently flowing water behind it, and then releasing it again into a rippling trickle from the sides.

"That's a beaver lodge there," he pointed. His constant, intelligent, and wanting-to-teach-me pointing finger was like a magic wand. He continued to explain just how the lodge was constructed, and—at that moment—a furry brown head with buck teeth poked out from the water momentarily and disappeared just as quickly. We both laughed and looked at each other briefly, acknowledging we'd seen the same thing.

The pines all around us stood proud and tall, bending ever so slightly in the fresh air's breeze. I felt like a fairy surrounded by a world too big for me. Below those trees, the ground looked like an endless field of green, scrubby, knee-high bushes all around. There were turtles, frogs, and snakes curiously coming out of their respective hiding spots to see who we were: one of which I picked up to investigate, and made Will stop, stare, hold his breath, and raise his eyebrows. He looked in equal parts shock and worry that I'd be bitten. I supposed he'd never seen a girl be so comfortable with nature, especially those of slime and slither. But I was in my element: good and dirty amongst wildlife. Back on the island, I'd always been one with creatures: crabs, fish, and all the slippery and stinky bait one could imagine. I enjoyed helping the animals caught in nets or washed up injured on the shoreline, too. Anything with feet, fins, feathers, or fur were always welcome, and I'd made the marina a little makeshift rescue shelter on the side.

He pointed out a little patch of cranberries that must have washed in from an over-flooded bog and taken up residence on the side of the stream. He couldn't figure out why it was already red, since harvesting season wasn't until autumn. *Maybe this day really was magic*, I thought. (Little did I know, he was thinking the same thing.) He picked a few, offered them to me, and nodded his head in a silent word of: "Go on, try it." Just like the trust I'd given him since the moment we'd met, I spit out my gum for a minute, and popped a berry in my mouth and chewed. It was very sour, and I spat it right back out. I looked at it in my hand, and it sort of resembled a miniature apple: red skin, white flesh, with little black seeds. My spitting sent him into great laughter, and when I watched him laugh, I couldn't do anything but be still and smile for a moment and then join right in. This day was turning out to be the best so far since I'd moved to this place of marvel. For the first time in almost a year, I was laughing.

There was an old, makeshift dock touching the water's edge, and we walked over to sit down. He continued to tell me about everything around us: the sounds, smells, views, and even the feel of lichen and moss. For hours, it was like living in a picture book, or perhaps even a scratch and sniff. He told me about the old cedar trees lining the waterways, the sweet pepperbush edging the trails that filled the air with a scent that lived up to their name, and the snapping turtles under the surface that we only knew were present by the tiny bubbles breaking the surface from time to time. He told me to look close so maybe I could see one, and—when I did—he slapped the water. This sent me flying back, which sent him flying into laughter.

I told him about the island, too, in little increments, and whenever my memories would become too much and remind me of my parents, I'd choke up a bit. At this, he'd always take over the conversation with lighter chit chat to make me feel comfortable. I could tell he cared about me, if even having only just met, and no one had ever looked at me the way he had either. I couldn't put my finger on it quite yet, but it made me feel safely harbored, and like I was the only person who mattered. In a few short hours, I'd become "his person," and I felt it deep in my bones. Trying to figure out this new relationship sometimes left me searching for words in my head, but always with a smile, too. Narby had always taken me for who I was, but now another person my own age did the same. I finally felt accepted.

For hours, we stayed on that dock. We laughed, told stories, and when we were hungry for lunch, he even shared half of a wrapped-bologna sandwich with me, which he pulled out of an over-sized pocket. I mentioned going back to the farmhouse to get food, but he didn't want me to leave. Truth be told, I didn't want to leave him either. Even if it was half a sandwich, it did the trick. We were more interested in playing anyway.

"Let's swim!" he proclaimed, after a few more hours passed and we'd finished poking around some holes in trees and turning over logs to look for fence lizards.

With a bit of regret, thinking I'd now miss the next phase of forest fun and let him down, I spoke softly with my head down, "I don't have anything to swim in."

"It's okay; no problem." He made me feel as if I could do no wrong. "We can just dip our feet." He had a way of making all things okay, and like I could never let him down. Some sort of super-human strength in the form of selfless courtesy.

"But I can run home to get it!" I said, perking up at my own idea, and innocently ignoring his last comment.

"No!" His abrupt and nervous order made me cock my head like one of the old seagulls on the island.

"Why not?" I replied, a bit taken aback.

He calmed, making sure he hadn't startled me too much and feeling a bit abashed. "Sunset is only an hour away. It looks really pretty through the woods, like a million twinkling stars coming down through the pine needles."

Had an entire day already gone by? I thought.

His tone then changed from tour guide to a bit more troubled, and he finally said out loud the words we'd both been thinking, "Besides, we'll probably have to go back home if they see us."

With his words coming out, it was like he was reading my mind: that we didn't want anyone to call us back to our respective homes for dinner [or the like], so our time together wouldn't end.

"Okay." I let the tips of my toes drift a bit with the soft current of the copper-colored water flowing by. After rolling up his jeans, he did the same. It was warm on the surface, but chilly the deeper I let my feet dangle.

The following moment touched me so deeply that I could feel it in my marrow. In a mature and confident manner that made this young boy appear to be a man, he spoke, "Katie, lay back on the dock and close your eyes, breathe deep, and listen." He spoke more quietly then. "When the wind blows, the pine needles whisper. And all together, they sound like the ocean washing up gently on the shore."

How he said it was so complete and poetic, romantic and breathtaking. In my mind, his words took me to the water's edge where I grew up. It was the sound I heard when first arriving, finally explained. Earlier, he had sensed my uneasiness when I spoke of the island, and the hurt he saw in my eyes was a longing. Somehow, he knew that. And while my eyes were still shut, I breathed deep smelling the sweet pine air of the forest around us, whispering like little waves. I could feel him watching me. And—still with my eyes closed—I smiled while I laid there knowing he was. I felt the connection between us like he did. It set a precedence that we'd always make each other feel alive, especially if we were feeling low. This moment was magic. Then and there, he brought me back to life. He filled the empty space inside me that I felt would never be whole again. I'd made my first real friend.

The sun finally started setting, and he was right: the light coming through the trees was so beautiful that it was hard to explain. We stayed until the last bits of it streamed through the needled branches and then followed the smaller zigzags of trails back toward the road we'd first met when it became dark. The sandy paths seemed to glow an eerie and beautiful white once the moon came out, and they were easy to follow. Nighttime was an entirely different feel. It was so quiet that I could hear my hungry tummy gurgling. It was a bit creepy, as if a creature would pop out from the low brush that edged right up alongside the paths. *Maybe a mutant chipmunk, unlike the cute one from earlier in the day.* The scarier my thoughts got, the more on edge with excitement I became. The sounds of owls dotted the canopy, and he noted the species of all the different calls. Squeaks in the bushes below revealed the dinner menu for the wise and winged ones above that would dine after we'd passed. A chill came over the air, and a darkness that I'd never seen before set in all around us. It seemed my new buddy was prepared, however, and he pulled out a little flashlight from his endless pockets. It was as if he lived for the excitement of these woods, and I was the lucky girl who'd found my perfect partner in adventure. We laughed and ran along beside each other, all while the thrill of creepiness lingered in the air. But it was cut short when we got back to the main road. There waiting for us was Narby, and a man by her side.

I'd learn right away the man was his dad, and he didn't look so happy; nor did Narby. Both stood with arms crossed and a questioning smug of disappointment on their faces. Though underlying, we could both sense they we're happy we'd found each other, too. We were clearly friends, but also a match in mischief. It was plain as day, perhaps written on our naughty faces, which… were also covered in sandy dirt and invisible germs collected during our outing.

Narby spoke, but his dad stayed silent. "Do you two realize what time it is? And how long you have been gone?"

We knew it was out of love and worry, but we were respectful enough to nod our heads shamefully, and Will even replied, "Yes ma'am." For some reason, he reminded me of a young cowboy. I couldn't quite place it yet, but his respect for all beings, his way of freedom, and his dress-style just fit the mold.

Her frown lightened, and his father grinned. All was silently forgiven.

"Come on, kids. Time for a late dinner." She gave us each a pat on our shoulders while they both shook their heads.

We walked off in the direction of the farm, with our corresponding guardians, but not before sneaking a glimpse of each other's faces: both full of devious grins and sparks in our eyes. This was going to be a good summer.

Falling asleep after an impromptu barbecue that night was tough. I wasn't just in a comatose state from burgers, sweet sun tea, baked beans, cornbread, and homemade peach pie, but—more so—in a state of restlessness: longing for morning to come quickly so I could get back out with Will to explore some more. He'd told me more stories of local legend and lore after dinner, while sitting under a big willow tree in Narby's yard. Fireflies had given a soft glow on his face while they clung to the breezy branches. Stories of creatures still unseen, mysterious monsters, and hidden graves of people long past. He seemed the expert on the area, and—given I was the newcomer—it seemed he couldn't tell, let alone show, me things fast enough.

As I laid there in my bed, I smelled the flowers he'd given me in a vase on my nightstand, and it was intoxicating. Between the sweet aroma, the racing thoughts, and a full belly, I finally fell into slumber. It was the most restful sleep I'd had in what seemed forever. I was finally at peace.

Chapter 5:

A Day on the Farm

The morning came as fast as I'd hoped, and I was out the screened porch door just as quickly after I ate breakfast, but not before a warning from the kitchen.

"Kate, don't go getting into too much trouble today," Narby hollered.

Not only was it a reminder of the prior night, I suppose she was thinking back to the time on the island when I'd buried one of the kids from school up to his neck in a sand pit I made on the beach. He had slingshot a seagull from the air, so it was only fair (or at least I thought it was) I put him in a partial, temporary grave. Though, the rising tide had not been in my plans. I didn't want to drown him—just teach him a good lesson: what it feels like to be as helpless as the bird he'd hurt. In the end, the fire department had to come to dig him out. As for myself: I was not allowed on the beach for a week, and my shovel was banned for the rest of summer.

"I promise!" I shouted distantly as I was running and already halfway down the front sandy path, so reminiscent of home. I knew Will would be waiting again, and waiting he was, with a snack.

"Whoa! They're huge!" my eyes widened at the sight of two peaches the size of croquet balls.

"From the farm my dad runs," he said with his head held high. Everything he spoke of in his life he was so proud of.

"Do you live on the farm?" I asked, somehow without having gotten this information in the last [less than] twenty-four hours.

"Yeah, we rent a house on the edge of the fields," he said, looking a little sheepish now. I could see in his mind that he compared me living in a huge old farmhouse (which I'd arrived at via shiny antique truck towing a beautiful, polished sailboat to complete the flamboyant entrance) to his modest life of renting. He was contrasting our lives internally, or the little we knew about each other's yet. There was still so much to learn and share, so that I did.

As we began to walk down the road, toward the path that would take us back to the dock, eating the juiciest and sweetest peaches I've ever tasted, it was my turn to tell him about my own childhood. I shared about the little bay shack I grew up in, especially to let him know that I, too, was from humble beginnings. All the way back to the water's edge, I told him about the bait shop and marina, Narby and my parents, our little island school, the warm sand and summer evenings. Finally, I told him about the storm. He became silent and still when I began, and when I was finished, he looked frozen. It was very unlike him to be so quiet, but I learned then he was also a good listener. He now fully understood why I'd been so distant and lost at times. It felt good to have finally shared my heartache out loud. It felt even better to have said it to *him*.

I figured after the solemn story, and as we approached the dock, it was a good time to let him know that today I'd come prepared.

"Look!" and I lifted my shirt to reveal my one-piece bathing suit.

At the note of this, he yelled, throwing a fist up into the air, "Woohoo!"

We chucked the peach pits blindly into the woods and began peeling off our clothes while we ran. Left then with only with our suits on, he grabbed my hand. No words were said, and we only needed to make eyes for a second, as if silently counting down to the grand jump. With his simple squeeze of my fingers, we went running and leaping

28

off the dock, and splashing into the waterhole. It was even cooler than expected when I went below the surface. When I bobbed back up with a bit of a chilly gasp, he chuckled, "You'll get used to it."

After splashing each other thoroughly, we decided to float with the current downstream a bit, and "a bit" became quite a while. Eventually, we realized it was too far to go back by swimming upstream. But with the abundance of trails, surely we'd find one soon enough if we climbed out on the bank, and that we did. Huffing from all our silly paddling, we dredged up the hill—a little more dramatic than probably warranted for a few kids—to the first trail we found. Luckily, a split in the path looked like it led back in the direction of the dock, so we headed that way. Once back to the dock, we started from where we'd leaped in the water, and followed our trail of strewn clothes back out of the woods again.

The walking in the forest would never get old. I'd learn throughout the summer that each day spent with Will would be filled with new discoveries of plants and animals, sounds, and scents. It really was enchanting, and—with the wizard of the pointing finger wand by my side—it was even more special. I was grateful, and I hoped he knew this.

Over the summer, he gave me the grand tour, most of the time leading me by my hand, which seemed to have become the norm, and it was welcomed. I had taken to his form of caring for me, and someone else taking the lead now and then. I had always been my own boss, carving my own path. But he carved it *with* me now and gave direction through each excursion. He was my equal. The grand tour of this particular day was to be on "his" farm.

The property he lived on was just as grand as Narby's, but even more well-kept—pristine even. Orchard trees were perfectly trimmed and in rows with no overgrowth hugging the trunks, flowers had their own little fields, and the blueberry bushes, amongst others, were flawlessly aligned. The colors of all the fruit and veggies were a rainbow for the eyes. In all my splendor, and his pride that had returned, he dropped my hand to let me take it all in.

"The farmers here have owned this property for hundreds of years," he proclaimed like a historian, still with the slight and unfounded western accent.

Now, I'd learned in the short while we'd come to know each other that he was one to exaggerate elaborately (mostly in efforts to impress me), but this information was, in fact, true, and I learned this as we approached the farm stand that was near the entrance to the farm. As we neared, I could see wooden crates of the peaches he'd met me with earlier in the day amongst an array of other earthly edibles. He pointed out signs from long ago, and black and white pictures from generations of the same family. Farm antiques lined the walls and shelves from days passed. He got so much satisfaction from sharing information as if they were his own family. As we walked along, one scent caught my nose, and he smiled as I sniffed. It was almost as he lived to show me new things that brought me joy.

"Cider donuts. Right this way, little lady." He took my hand again for a moment just for direction, and off we went toward the bakery inside the stand.

I found it funny how he treated me like I was younger, as if to be my guardian and the more mature partner in this new relationship. Somehow, his life had created him this way, so perhaps he just was. His maturity was beyond his years, and he fit just right in his own world and skin. He took me into that world little by little, and I was happy to become a part of it.

When entering a little bakery, a few elderly women, maybe sisters or old friends, turned to us. I eventually went with the former guess seeing the similar smiles, kindness, and motions that they were in fact all related somehow.

"Well, hello kids," they hollered kindly in our direction. "Perfect timing!"

He nodded for me to follow. We headed to the counter, and his boyish arms reached for the sugary offerings handed our way. Warm apple cider donuts, fresh from the oven. The smell alone knocked me off my feet, but the taste was right on par with the peaches. *How was everything in this small town so wonderful?* I thought to myself. It really was the land of magic that Narby had always talked about, and now I understood. One sweet surprise after another. The natural beauty here was charming, the people were kind, and the flavors of the town from food, colors, and sounds were welcoming.

He started up [in his somewhat western voice again], "These folks here are my farm family."

This accent of his must have been imported with the handmade cowboy boots he got as a birthday gift from Wyoming, which he'd told me about in our montage of a conversation while floating downstream. I liked his voice. It was charming and fit him perfectly. Everything about him was unique, and suitable.

With warm welcomes and introductions all around, I learned that the ladies had already been made aware of my coming, and they commented on how nice it was for Will to finally have a friend his own age. This remark of theirs referred to him always tagging along behind the farmer's son, about five years older than Will and me. Although they all loved the little blond cowboy, there was more intense work to be done that only the farmer's son could tend to, so Will being around was sometimes a [loving] hindrance to Randy. And this "Randy" walked in right at that moment. It seemed that every time the donuts were made, the folks in the fields followed their noses to come in for a bite.

"Heya," he gave Will a rub on the head like a little brother, but Will stood straight, almost seeming to stand his ground on an even playing field, especially after he saw my face turn a shade of pink as this handsome farmer's son strolled over to us.

Instead of a rub on the head for me as well, and regardless that I had damp, cropped and frayed jeans on, he reached for my hand to shake gently, and said, "Nice to meet you, Kate." *He knew my name!*

Will was jealous, if even my attention on Randy was momentary, but I missed seeing this. I guess the ladies saw though, and giggled.

Will made short of the bakery visit to get me back all to his own and told me he'd give me the grand tour. Off to explore the property we went.

The first sight that caught my eye was a John Deere tractor heading our way. In passing, the driver looked down at Will as if with a special spot in his heart just for him and tilted his light-colored cowboy hat. He wore denim, button-down shirt with jeans of a similar shade. Perhaps this is where Will captured his sweet, wanna-be western persona. In turn, Will tipped his cap right back.

"That's Farmer Russ," Will said, as he stood smiling off behind the tractor as it passed. His head held high.

I smiled, unnoticed by Will from the side, internally giggling at him as he was still pleased with his moment of fame for being noticed by the head of the farm.

He told me how the farmers were getting a bit older, and hence the reason for his dad taking over the full-time job of manager and them renting the little farmhouse on the edge of the property. Randy would be entering high school that year and wouldn't have enough time to help as much anymore, so Will's dad was a perfect match. Their families had been friends for years anyway, so it was only natural to help each other out. Just like back on the island, people here seemed to have it in their blood to take care of one another.

"Com'on!" His voice was never faltering when he spoke of a new plan, and this time, it was one of running through the freshly turned fields.

Although sandy, it was mixed with enough soil to give it the rich appearance of the fertile farming earth that it was. Before we stepped into the field, he looked at me and wiggled his eyebrows up and down twice. This, of course, signaled the unspoken bedlam between us that had started our swim earlier. We had at it.

Shoes already off from our quest in the woods, we took off full speed through the field, kicking up as much dirt as possible, and "assisting" in the field work. Running and screaming every time the tractor made a turn to come our way, we could see Farmer Russ's warm smile behind the window. It turned into a game that lasted quite a while. Our damp clothes became caked in mud, and any bit of exposed skin was covered in grime as well.

We eventually tired of the zooming around, and when our feet were good and brown, we headed to a shady spot under a grove of red oaks that lined the field. Backs up against a tree, we laughed and huffed. It'd been a good romp, and the day was still young. In his own jean pockets, always prepared for the unknown, he pulled out a little brown paper bag. It was all rolled up resembling an over-cooked summer sausage, but enough to see it was filled with something else. Out he pulled some venison jerky. He told me his dad was a hunter, and he shot the deer that the dried meat came from. As an animal lover, my nature was to reject the offering, but I couldn't be rude, nor let him down in his effort to introduce me to something new. Besides, I could sense by the story he told me as he unwrapped the snack that the hunting was more of a family tradition than a sport. He told me they used the meat and shared it with others in the town, much like we'd shared food at our storm parties on the island. He explained that hunting was better than buying meat at the grocery store.

"Instead of caging an animal its entire life and then ending it with a slaughter, the deer are able to roam free, and be killed quickly," he said. "In the end, the head, and even the body sometimes, is preserved by the local taxidermist to remember the great creature that shared itself with us."

As he explained this, contemplation ran through me. He was nothing short of a man, just… shorter! His ways of explanation, patience, and educating those about things he took pride in, were well-established in his soul.

The jerky was more a labor of chewing, but tasty all the same. He found it so amusing when I just went along with whatever came my way. Whether I acted like a tomboy or the girl I was, he put it like this right then and there, "You're pretty well-rounded, you know." Then, after a slight pause, he couldn't help but blurt out, "… and… pretty." He shied at this last comment of his, as if he didn't mean for it to slip out. I suppose he figured then was the best time to say it as he now had competition from the farmer's son.

I about choked while gnawing and couldn't have imagined a more inappropriate time to say such a thing actually; mostly because I was covered in dirt, and must have now smelled like meat, mud, and sweat.

I just turned to look at him and smiled shyly in return. Which was unlike me to be shy, but he made me feel like a girl for the first time in my life. The romantic gesture on his end turned to a dry mouth on mine, and I couldn't quite reply to say thank you as intended. After all the running and the dehydrating treat, I was parched. He could see I was too. From an extra-deep jean pocket, he pulled a little flask.

"Have some, Katie," he said caringly, reaffirming he liked my full name, as he passed it first to me, before considering even a sip for himself. Somehow, the water was cold in his little canteen, even after having been in his jeans running through a hot field. It was perfectly timed and hit the spot.

"Thank you, Will, and… thank you for saying I'm pretty," I replied quietly, for [finally] both the compliment and the drink. Like the tomboy I was, I started to wipe my mouth with the back of my hand, but this time, I caught myself. For once, my desire to be more lady-like had surfaced, and I was a bit ashamed for using a body part, and not a napkin [had it been present], to wipe my wet lips. I hid my wiping and did it quickly; swearing in my head I needed to learn better manners.

After sharing and finishing off the water, he told me of the great underground aquifer that ran below the Pine Barrens.

"It's the cleanest, and freshest water you'll ever taste, and that's exactly what's in there", as he pointed to the flask. "It's why it's so cold down at the water hole. It's always coming up from below, and always fresh."

He continued about the water systems, followed by local history, and more of the folklore from the previous night.

Amid a story, a voice from behind called out, "Hey, you two!"

It was Randy again. I must have blushed, and Will straightened up protectively once more.

"Hi," I grinned, maybe even overly zealous.

Will was not having any of this. Not a bit. He stood up complacently as quickly as he could, and as he did—the last bits of water from the flask spilled between his legs, making it appear as though he'd wet his jeans, that had finally dried from being wet after our swim.

Randy and I both grunted a slight laugh. I laughed because I felt I was laughing *with* the handsome guy, not *at* my friend. But Will saw it as being the target of a bad joke. He picked up the jerky bag gently from the ground between us and walked off, seeming truly hurt. It was almost as if to let us know he was offended that we could even think of putting him down, when he cared so deeply for us both: one like a big brother, and one like a new girl he (very clearly now) had a crush on. I felt bad. It was charming and especially because he'd only known me for a short time, and now I'd hurt his feelings.

Randy just shook his head, and yelled after Will as he stormed off, "Okay, see ya then!"

Randy then looked at me, winked, and walked off. He was back to collecting strawberry crates that employees had been picking all day to load into a wagon attached to another tractor. I was off in my own direction to find Will.

By the time I made it back to the farm store, backtracking slowly the whole way to scan each area of the farm closely, I'd not seen Will, and it appeared he was nowhere to be found. I guess he'd recently passed through though, as the women, finishing up the last batch of donuts for the day, smiled out of the corner of their mouths while they snuck a glance at me in my search. I pretended not to see, but at least I felt better knowing he'd been seen. I was shocked at my feelings for being so worried that I couldn't find him. My worry continued a bit until I stepped out a door leading back to the field. There Will was, in all his proud glory, driving the tractor. Farmer Russ was now the one watching from the side and giving Will the thumbs up as he drove right past me: smugly not looking an inch my direction. He knew I was there, of course, but I'd been shunned… at least for the day.

Chapter 6:

THE SMELL OF ICE CREAM

The next morning started off as usual, and the previous day's antics had all been silently pardoned as if nothing had ever happened in the first place. Time really flew by when we were having fun, and not letting anything get in the way. In fact, the rest of the summer seemed to pass quickly: wild, water-logged, and with lots of wandering. By August, we were inseparable and best friends, for sure. This month also brought a bit of change to town: the annual festival. Food, rides, music, and games would be waiting for us, and we needed to prepare—respectfully as kids would. This was *very* important.

As the town we lived in was small, we'd be allowed to go alone, of course. Everyone looked out for one another, and we'd be safe. Besides, it was right across the lane from the farm where Will lived and set up on an empty field rented out by the farmers.

One night just before my birthday, Will came to Narby's to pick me up by the gate so we could walk together. Before we could start walking, though, he took out a box from behind his back. It was wrapped in rainbow construction paper that had been taped together and tied with hay bale twine.

"Go ahead, open it!" he said.

When I pulled the string off and pushed the lid aside, there was a pair of cowgirl boots. They were the same brown leather as Will's, but with flowers embroidered on the sides. I couldn't believe my eyes! I thought it was such a sweet gesture, and without thought, I placed the box on the ground, and threw my arms around him with thanks.

"Happy birthday, Katie," he said, with my arms still around his neck, hugging me back. "Narby told me your size."

I had no idea he knew it was my special day.

Pulling away, I smiled, and said, "These are so pretty! Thank you, Will!"

He grinned from ear to ear, pleased with himself that I was pleased too. I think I saw him blush again like he often did these days, but I pretended not to notice.

"I got them at the tack store in the next town. Not from Wyoming, but they *are* real leather!" he piped up.

I knew he must have spent all his allowance to buy them, and I wasn't sure how else to show my thanks. I just kept smiling, and he looked so proud that we were matching.

I smiled at Will, "Wait here. I'm going to go get some socks!"

I ran into the house, deciding to replace my flip flops with the boots (the boots being the better choice to stomp around festival grounds in anyway), and ran back out.

"They look great! You're officially a country girl." He was proud and beaming.

I finally felt like I fit in somewhere—if not in school, by Will's side.

When we arrived at the fair, it was in full swing. A bit like the wild frolicking from the farm field from the beginning of summer, we darted into the abyss of popcorn-scented air, flashing ride lights, and life-size music box sounds. For the local kids, it was an annual event that meant a change of scenery. We had nothing of the sort on the island, so for me it wasn't just a backdrop—but an entirely new experience.

Our first stop was for food. I'd eaten cotton candy before, of course, but not the way Will did. He pulled me to stand downwind of the machine.

"Stick out your tongue," he directed, and little spider webs of sweet sugar blew into my mouth. I thought it was a divine idea, until sugar blew into Will's eyes, and he brought his hands to them to rub. It was only momentary worry that went through my head that he was hurt because his giggle calmed it all. He just had a way about him that made every little bit of life larger and more joyful, and nothing to get upset about. We just stuck to eating the sugary treat with our hands after that and not trying to lick it from the air.

We had ten dollars each, so we needed to be selective. Choices of games, sweets, and rides were tough decisions, so we put deep thought into the picking. First, we decided on the Tilt-a-Whirl. We figured we'd get the wild rides out of the way first, so we didn't get sick on them later after eating junk. These teacups with a half umbrella hood spun and bounced as if over a long bumpy road—but ten times faster and wilder. I was grateful at this moment to have chosen cotton candy and not corn dogs.

Will's laughter never got old, and he clearly felt the same as I did. There were moments amid our laughter that his voice would go from a shrilling giggle, to a warm smile, to just watching me for short moments, though his current stare was cut short when our heads were smashed together at the sides from the force of twirling gravity. But the gravity wasn't strong enough to keep his hands away from mine, as he snuck one of them over to my own and placed it palm down over the top of my knuckles. I couldn't quite figure out how such a small gesture of protection and affection could make my stomach flutter more than the wild ride did, but I felt something strong for this boy, and it warmed me. That moment changed something between us.

When the ride stopped and the gravitational pull vanished, we didn't get up right away, but turned our heads just enough that our noses touched. I wasn't quite sure what the moment would bring, but my breath caught, and I became unmoving. Whatever it was, it was cut short by a man missing a few teeth and the rest filled with grit and saliva from his tobacco chew, scolding us to "Move along!"

We made eye contact for a moment, and at that time I felt the same way he felt about me. He was my person too. We laughed and got out of the ride and walked away holding hands.

With our newfound connection, I initiated even more of a drive to act ladylike. But not before following through with a plan I'd already prepared.

"Wanna get some ice cream?" I asked, completely void of any impending guilt.

"Yeah!" he returned.

We walked up to the little cart, and Will got out his little leather wallet that matched his boots. In his never-ceasing cowboy and mannerly style, he ordered two soft-serve vanilla cones with rainbow jimmies and handed me one.

"For the birthday gal," he winked.

We wandered over to a patch of grass to sit away from the circus-like chaos, for a moment of rest and nibbling our tasty treats. For a little while, we just licked the frozen goods, and then I found it hard to keep the image of my plan out of my head. I could barely take it anymore, so it was now or never.

"Will, this ice cream smells really good!" I said.

Without second thought, he leaned in for a sniff, and I shoved the bottom of his cone right up into his face. He turned to me in complete shock, raised eyebrows over his widened eyes, and a gaping mouth. Priceless.

"Gotta look out for those snapping turtles," I said coyly with a cheesy grin and squinty eyes, to note the payback I'd been planning since the day we met, and he'd splashed me with water.

As his face returned to a devilish grin, almost outdoing my own, I realized he found this a challenge. (I still found it hilarious.) We snickered, as he licked the melted cream from around his lips, and then wiped the rest from his nose with the side of his hand.

"Well, okay. I deserved that. But now you're on!" he grinned.

"Oh yeah? What's the challenge?" I asked.

"Let's go play some games. I've been coming here my whole life playing these games. I don't think you'll ever beat me on any. Not once." I loved how he emphasized "whole," as if his life had already been so long. He really was an old soul.

My grin was answer enough. As we crunched down the rest of the sugar cone bottoms, we headed back into the hometown crowd toward the frog launch. It was simple: frog on one end of a seesaw-looking apparatus, area to hit with a mallet on the other end, and lily pads in the middle of a make-shift pond to land the slimy, rubber amphibious toys.

"Now, I'll have you know, this takes muscle," he said and I could see the challenge starting.

He rolled up the sleeves of his already short-sleeved plaid shirt, showing some muscle, alright. Although he was young, I did see the strength. From working on the farm, he really was strong. It was apparent when he slugged the first target, made the frog leap, and it landed well at the far end of the pond in front of us. The splash came with a comment too.

"Eww! Will! Can't you keep your germs to yourself?" It was Kitty. Oh just great. *Lucky us.*

We just looked at each other and rolled our eyes, but she was ready to sink the claws.

She continued, pushing for rebuttal, "What? Too much of a gentleman in front of your *girlfriend* to talk back to me?" She emphasized the girlfriend part, as she yelled from across the water.

We tried to ignore her.

"You're as slimy as that frog, Will. Just a kid who likes to play in the mud," she said and scowled, pushing harder for a fight.

For some reason, it seemed to get to Will, and I could see his jaw clench a little as he looked away.

Instead of waiting for him to answer, I made a change in my avoiding her right then and there. As she turned away back into the fair and giggled with her posse of nasty girlfriends, I grabbed a frog that was next in line for launching, winked at Will, and scurried through the crowd separating us from her. I snuck up behind Kitty and her snarky gaggle and put the soaking wet frog right down the back of her shirt. She shrilled and her friends all put their hands over their mouths, gasping.

"Oh gross! GROSS!" she said, mortified.

I had the final say, "Who's the slimy one now, Kitty?"

I tilted my head, grinned, made my eyes into thin threatening lines, and spun around: walking away to leave her horror struck and with a big wet spot on the back of her preppy monogrammed shirt.

When I got back around the booth to Will, he shook his head, and smiled, also maybe a little in shock. We were on the same page. We just got each other. There was no other way to put it: we just got each other.

"I guess the boots brought out the cowgirl in me," I said, pleased with myself, and even happier that Will was smiling with so much dignity.

I suppose he felt it necessary to regain his manly pride, so he took my hand, and off to a new stop we headed. This time: the corn crate contest.

A bunch of grown men, with Randy thrown into the mix, stood around a circle of hay bales, each with twenty stacked and unmade corn crates on top. A man on a chair, most likely the brother of the half-toothed hillbilly from the whirling ride, held an air horn. Will marched up alongside the other men and made himself right at home. I was left behind with the other spectators and saw a wooden bench next to the ladies I recognized from the farm. They smiled at me and patted next to them on the empty seat to come take the spot.

Almost seeming to have inside information, they looked at me grinning. And when I looked back at Will, he was also grinning, from ear to ear, and shook his head a few times up and down when he looked at me.

Everyone waited for a few more men to take their places, a few rules to be shouted out, and then a countdown. With a shrilling honk from the air horn, the crate assembling began, and the crowd cheered.

With straw flying everywhere, people standing and clapping only a few seconds into the racket of the wood and wire, I'd almost lost sight of him. A short time later, the cheering climbed to an outright roar, and I looked up to see to men hoisting Will in the air on their shoulders.

"And for the third season in a row, young Will gets the trophy for assembly in less than a minute!" *That was the fastest contest I ever saw!*

After a few pats on the back from fellow farmers, Will casually came over to put his trophy down and took my hand after some country music started. *Seriously? He could dance too?*

I was quick to stand my ground, "Oh no. No sir. I do not dance." I shook my head, terrified at the notion to boogie to country swing and the array of songs coming from the string band.

"Have it your way. But at least watch, and then maybe if you learn the steps, you'll be brave enough to try it out." He winked, knowing his emphasis of the word "brave" might rattle me enough to come out and prove him wrong. But I shook my head no. He shook his head back at me—smiling—and then went to the dance floor, still covered in bits of straw.

He danced his heart out right then and there, next to men and women, and other kids with the nerve—never missing a beat, nor a chance to glance at me to make sure I was watching. But my watching was overcome by shear shock—and surprise jealousy—when Kitty showed up by his side.

It must have been gentleman-etiquette not to turn down a lady (or a witch), because when she snuck a malevolent glance at me and offered her hand to him, he took it! My hand. His hand was my hand to hold. I was floored at the image, floored at my feelings, and even more floored at how far Will would go just to be the bigger person and make peace, if, in fact, peace was what he was aiming for. I was so confused. There they were, hand in hand, dancing! She'd just verbally taunted him less than ten minutes prior (and for his whole life as he'd once told me), not to mention tried to destroy me in class the previous school year, and now here they were: dancing to something I wouldn't even know how to move to without stepping on my own feet. Watching them western-style waltz made me feel a little lost and alone again. For the first time that summer, I was taken back to half a year earlier, when I first stepped into the classroom, and knew I didn't belong. I supposed I still didn't. Standing there in cowgirl boots, I just felt plain dumb. I lowered my head in part longing, loneliness, and a sense of feeling sheepish for having thought I'd truly ever fit in. I looked slowly from side to side, and just felt left out, abandoned, and embarrassed, and turned gradually to stand and mosey off in my own grief. The farm ladies even looked shocked at the whole scene, but almost seeming to know something I didn't, information that they, nor anyone else, had control over. They looked sad for me and understood my feeling awkward. I supposed the night was over for me, so I just started heading home.

I thought for a few minutes Will would realize I was missing as he'd looked over at me so many times before Kitty had swept in. But the few times I looked back before slipping out of the crowd, he was just focused on his dance moves and looking down at his feet. He wasn't looking at her like everyone else at their partners, but he wasn't walking away either. I was though. I was done for the night, and was walking as far away as I could.

I made it back to the road that led away from the festival and would pass the farm and eventually lead back to Narby's. I kicked a few stones with my boots. *Stupid boots. Should have just worn my flips after all.*

The further I got from the festival and the closer to the early August corn fields I got, the quieter it became. The warm soothing breeze of the summer, and the fireflies still looming around in the fields was something to relax about now. Maybe it wasn't about the people here after all, and just the place itself was something to keep hope in. The festival noise was replaced with the sounds of crickets and distant cicadas, and the air smelled more of damp earth from the nighttime dew than fried sugar and popcorn. Maybe I didn't need a friend or anyone at all. Maybe the town itself would fill my void. But at that thought, I started to feel sad again, and zoned out in longing. I was all but lost in the peaceful atmosphere and my own thoughts, when an arm grabbed me and just about made me collapse from surprise.

"Why'd ya leave?" It was Will and he was upset, at least by the look on his face in the moonlight.

"Well, why do you think?" I asked, this time upset in my own right, and downright disappointed.

He knew what I meant and offered the explanation immediately.

"Katie, my dad works on her parents' farm sometimes for extra money," looking ashamed again. "If she tells her dad I was rude or mean, my dad might get fired. Her parents give her anything she wants." He looked so desperate, disappointed in himself, and exasperated trying to explain. It was clear he was afraid he'd ruined our bond. This also explained the looks on the old farm ladies' faces earlier. Kitty and her family were known for being rude, and the whole town knew it.

The comfort of knowing that he did what he did out of burden rather than desire made me feel more at ease. He hated having to explain and talk about her. I could tell. But I wasn't quite finished with my own thoughts, so I chimed in.

"She was mean to us just before you danced. She was mean to us the entire time either of us have known her! And you just forget it like that? I know you said you had to, but you didn't frown when you were with her either, you know." I had a sour look on my face.

When he attempted to answer, I just turned my head and continued walking.

"I… I can't explain… you have to believe…," he tried saying and reached at my arm as I kept walking away.

I guess my guard dropped a bit when I felt his gentle hand find mine again. *My hand.* I took a deep breath of relief but kept it quiet so he wouldn't hear it.

I had to make peace now and forgive him. It was the right thing to do, especially for such a good soul. "It's okay. Maybe I do believe you, maybe I don't." It was a changing of position, and this time I was the one that'd be asked of forgiveness in a sense. Just like I'd been punished for having made fun of him that day on the farm with Randy, I'd perhaps milk this one a bit to my advantage and punish him, too. But I didn't have the heart. I'd never ask him to apologize. He'd woken up the morning after he'd spilled his water on his pants already having forgiven me and made the rest of the summer so memorable for me, too. He had wanted this night to be special and unforgettable as well, and here I was walking away from everything he'd worked so hard on planning. I saw dishonor and hurt in his eyes, and I felt bad for being the one who brought it on him. Kitty or not, there was no reason to fuss over something I knew he was being honest about—and I was being dramatic about. No reason to hurt such a good human.

"Anyway, I do," I said, hoping he'd ask what.

"Do what?" he did ask after all.

"Believe you. And sorry I left," I said and put my head down now, feeling my own shame now.

"I was just worried about you. I mean, you just left and went off into the dark." His protective worry was back. It made my guilt of bringing that humiliated look over his face even heavier in my gut.

"Want to catch some lightening bugs?" I said, trying my best to lighten the mood.

And just like that, the flash of life returned to his blue eyes, and— once again—all had been forgiven.

He chuckled a faint *he he he*, and out from a deep pocket of his trousers, he pulled a handful of firecrackers, completely disregarding the idea of chasing bugs.

Always prepared, I thought.

"I almost forgot I had these!" he said, looking pleased with himself.

"Where'd you get those?" I squealed with delight.

"Randy! He gave them to me for winning the corn crate contest before I left. We have a bet every year, and every year he gives me a prize if I win." He held out his hand, to reveal a few noisy and fiery varieties of miniature explosives.

"And how are we gonna light those?" I inquired.

"Matches. I asked Farmer Russ for some at the farm. He didn't ask what I needed them for, so I didn't tell him."

Farmer Russ knew exactly why he'd wanted them. Will was a good kid; mischievous, but good. He was not going to use them to hurt any-one nor cause property damage. He just wanted a little old-fashioned, summer fun.

Oh, good gosh, this boy really *was* my partner in crime. Now, I knew why Narby and his dad had those humble reservations in the beginning.

Without further explanation, I was put in charge of lining them up on the ground, and he oversaw lighting.

The first "popper" didn't go off. So, we thought lighting the entire handful in a whole bunch might work better. He lit a match and dropped it into our mini, makeshift, bonfire-looking pile, and they took alright. Popping and flying all over, we had to dive into a corn row to avoid getting whacked with one. Of course, they were tiny, so they'd have not done much harm anyway (probably the reason Randy handed them over to Will in the first place), but we made the moment big, and dove for cover. We got dirtier and louder with each one we set off, as he kept pulling more from different jean pockets. *Those bottomless, treasure trove, jean pockets.* So, by the time we were all out, it was a bit sad knowing the fun was over.

But it wasn't. From tucked in his boot, Will pulled out sparklers. He handed me two and kept two for himself. *Kid was like a vault of goodies!*

He stated, "I'm going to light all four and then we have to race to the end of the rows. First one to the other side wins."

Once they were lit, off we went. The ground was hardened from the prior hot weeks, and bumpy from where the tractors had passed in the last rain before that. This created an obstacle and a few falls too. But we kept laughing and running after each recovery, somehow keeping the sparklers' flame from disappearing. By the time we hit the end, almost exactly at the same time, our little sparkling sticks had fizzled out, and we were left with only the moonlight to see by. At least, we were back in the open and not in the dark corn rows where the moonlight would have been dim. Far enough from the festival now, the only noises were the crickets again, distant tree frogs, owls, and the corn stalks rustling on each other in the slight breeze. The grass had grown in a nice low and soft space in the adjoining fallow field, so we walked out. Once in the center, we slumped to the ground to lay and catch our breath. Side by side—his hands behind his head, and mine on my belly—we stared up into a clear sky. It was another reminder of the island. Some nights, I'd snuck out from the marina, and walked up to the dunes to the ocean-side just to lie on the sand and look up. I thought about my parents then. But just as my eyes were about to tear up, I saw a shooting star. Will saw it too.

"Whoa! D'ja see it?" he blurted out.

"Yeah," but I spoke more calmly than his excited question. He just lay quietly, sensing my moment of peace, and I smiled. Looking up at the sky, my memory of my parents brought happiness for the first time, rather than pain. More so, I was glad to have this feeling overcome me, with my Will by my side. My person. From the moment we'd met, we were friends. But now, he was, no doubt, my person.

We laid there for quite a while and counted the shooting stars. It was if they were putting on a show just for us that night.

He reached over the grass to hold my hand and whispered in my ear, reminding me I was most important to him, "Happy Birthday, Katie."

Chapter 7:

THE JERSEY DEVIL

The following years were repeats of those passed: gallivanting in the woods and at the waterhole, spending time at each other's homes for picnics, enjoying the festival each year, and avoiding Kitty… even if it wasn't gentleman-like for Will. He'd found ways to evade her without jeopardizing his dad's work, and she was too involved with her fancy horse shows and snobby girlfriends to really take notice anyway. Of course, most of our time was spent doing things here and there on the farm. We became closer than ever, and over those years, I'd also gotten to know an older man named Mr. Leeds. Will had introduced us, of course.

He was a local and an old farm friend, and always welcomed to come and ride around on the farm to "inspect." He was a veteran of the U.S. military, and here on the farm, he was given the respect he deserved and earned: the freedom to do as he pleased with his retirement, for all the years he'd served selflessly to keep us free in our own country. He did this daily inspection on a make-shift lawnmower he'd rebuilt himself. But the most noted oddity of this quiet man was his pet skunk, which no one knew had stink glands or not. This creature made for a sort-of bodyguard dressed in his own little professional black and white suit. Its name was "Mr. Mayor" and it always rode in a basket Mr. Leeds had attached to the side of the mower. Mr. Leeds always wore overalls with a long-sleeved white shirt under it: no matter how hot the temperature. The skin on his hands was weathered, and beneath his shirt, you could see the muscle from days past—perhaps from days he worked so hard fighting in wars long gone. Just as Narby had entertained me with stories growing up, Mr. Leeds had always entertained Will just the same.

One day in spring, after a short stint of weeding in the fields to prepare for the season, Mr. Leeds joined us under one of the oak trees for lunch. And boy did he have a story to tell alright!

The Jersey Devil is quite possibly the most notorious monster of the Pinelands. Dating back as far as anyone telling the story will share: its eyes are glowing red, it's llama-looking with a long neck stemming from a leathery horse body and standing upright on two cloven-hoofed back feet. It has huge wings, and twisted horns that resemble black licorice to complete the horrid look. Most of these stories (although ever-changing) come from the people of this area, called "Pineys." They are proud folks, just like on island, and now I knew the reason for the name of Narby's boat. They had "Piney Power," and it was a way of stating that they were a force to be reckoned with. Mr. Leeds was a perfect example of these folks, with his stern face full of insight and waggishness. His heart and soul were born from these woods, and he was proud of it.

All day we spent hearing of this creature, so it was an [unspoken] no-brainer to head straight for the woods at dark and begin our own search. This impending excitement made for day-long, sneak-attack giggles, and a longing like no other.

By the time dinner was done, and the sun finally set, we were given permission by our guardians to take our flashlights, be safe, and have fun. We made our promises, and off we went. Will was like a seasoned forest guide at this point, and Narby and his father felt I'd gotten to know the woods enough over the years as well, that we'd be fine for a bit on our own without a curfew.

Unlike a night with a full moon to light our walk, the sky was hidden above a blanket of low-lying clouds, seeming to keep secrets hidden in them. *Would it rain? Would the sky mysteriously open revealing a soft glowing and eerie twilight? Would ghastly arms reach down from the clouds to brush the top of our hair as we walked beneath them?*

Our outing began on our usual sandy road, and off we went to hit the trails. Only this time, we'd take the path unknown. This was nothing the adults knew about, of course, but it just added to the thrill. This trail, as it turned out, was a trail Will had never ventured on alone: day or night. He was always told to avoid this route, as it snaked more windingly than the others, and split off into too many directions that might make for a difficult return. Not only that; this was a place he feared a bit. I didn't realize this 'til his holding my hand was more for his own security than a place of leading me for once. It made me a little nervous, but the anticipation of adventure hid the fear, and we trudged on. His terror was a comical one in a way, especially when his voice would crack with nervousness when trying extra hard to act valiant.

In a move of bravery (or maybe to challenge his own), Will directed us to turn at the first split in the trail, aiming us to the unfamiliar territory. It was a tighter fitting path than our regular route to the waterhole, and rough, ground-level plants brushed at our ankles. We had to follow each other in a row rather than side by side, and even though I could tell Will was scared, he let me stay in front and he stayed in the back. Every now and then, I could tell he was looking behind to see if anything was following because he'd stumble off the trail a bit, making the low scrubby shrubs rustle, and my hand wobble a bit. It'd make me giggle, under my breath, of course.

The further we went into the woods, the darker it got, and the more untouched it became. Shining our flashlights all around us lit up a whole new place full of unharmed space and old growth. The trails weren't flattened and worn bare like those blazed on the main course. These were trails only taken by the brave, and the locals, like deer, raccoons, and, apparently on this night, us. The deeper we went, the quieter it became too. Every branch we stepped on cracked and echoed out into the forest around us. If the breeze blew a bit in the treetops, our minds went directly past the usual ocean-washed sound and focused on the creaking of the branches and trunks instead. Tonight, was a perfectly creepy night for the hunt, and something loomed in the clouds that I couldn't quite put my foot on just yet.

Ahead on the trail, we noticed a low-hanging branch. But it wasn't the branch that caught our attention. It was a chain coming down from it. We stopped dead in our tracks when the inch-round interloped metal lowered slowly, then seemed to slide side to side on the branch. It'd have been enough to make us turn around and run back right then and there if it hadn't been for the numbness that now ran through our veins, making us freeze in our tracks. Continuing to stare at the chain and slowly moving our eyes upwards on it, hands clenched tightly together now, we noticed a foot attached to it, a large bird foot! As we noticed this, a giant rooster dropped from the branch and charged toward us squawking. Had it not been for its short metal leash, he'd surely have poked our eyes out. We screamed. The moment spooked us, but the humor in the bird's charging cleared the air of fright, and laughter soon broke out in our usual sense. We fell over each other in a way to keep from collapsing to the ground, roaring in hysterics. The rooster looked highly offended. And with that, he made a short fly-hop action back into his perch. We had yet to figure out why this bird was chained up, and, although we had a sense of sadness for its captivity as a Piney security system, we dared each other to run under it to cross to the other side.

"One, two, three!" we counted together, and then darted under the branch, continuing the great quest.

Having passed by the weird fowl and a bit out of breath from adrenaline and the sprint, we slowed to a leisurely pace, and Will held my hand once we were side by side again when the trail opened a bit more.

"Long ago, this was a place Indians settled. One day we can dig, and we'll find arrowheads," he said, speaking like a historian again.

"Arrowheads?" I was clueless.

"They're these flat, triangle things sometimes the size of a dog paw. They're really sharp, and they would put them on the end of sticks to hunt stuff."

(It was the "stuff" part that let my mind wander.)

He continued, "The Indians had lots of cool tools and rituals, too. They say when Indians died, they kept the families together in grave circles."

"What do you mean?" I asked, part freaked out and part curious.

"I guess they thought it was a way to keep the families together forever. When a family member would die, they'd plant a pine bush over where they got buried, and continue the circle until it was complete, until all those in that immediate family were gone… *at least in this world*." He ended this last comment with a ghastly tone to spook me, which, he thoroughly enjoyed when he saw it did.

I was unsure if this was one of his romanticized tales, but he sure seemed adamant that this was all fact.

He spoke again, "So keep your eyes peeled. Maybe we'll find an old burial plot."

I was under the impression we were hunting the Jersey Devil, but the addition of the graves upped the ante and had the hairs on my arms sprouting from their respective mini mounds of goosebumps. We were enjoying the adventure, and for two kids like us, it meant scaring the heck out of each other the best way possible.

Up ahead, there was an opening in the clouds that allowed the moon to shine down on a small meadow of sorts. It was beautiful, but still that lingering sense of the unknown was ever so present. Will nodded to follow, and we stepped out to the side of the clearing. We looked out into the field, like two deer looking to steer clear of hunters during open season.

Once we walked out to the center, a creepy fog rolled in quickly, and covered the field and our legs from the knees down. It reminded me of something, but I couldn't quite place it yet. Whatever it was, it made my stomach start to churn, and I became truly nervous.

As the breeze picked up a bit, and as fast as the fog had rolled in, it blew off into the forest again, disappearing into the black of the night. The moon was shining now, and the clearing more visible. Maybe I had nothing to be nervous about after all, but I was left shivering. We looked around, turning in slow circles, realizing it would be time to walk back soon. But the direction we'd be going would be difficult to choose as it was clear we had gotten a bit turned around, and downright lost. I felt confident with Will by my side that wherever we ended up we'd be okay because we had each other. But my confidence was challenged when I realized he looked as lost as we really were.

We checked down at our feet to make sure the fog had completely cleared so we could walk again without tripping but noticed something. As we turned around slowly, we realized we were standing in the middle of a perfect circle: seven pine shrubs. We were standing in the middle of a burial plot! If the rooster from earlier wasn't enough to make our blood run cold, it was now frozen in our veins.

At the same time the notion kicked in that we were standing at the center of an ancient cemetery, darkness fell around us again, and the moon was quickly shut out by darker and thicker clouds. A rumbling began, and it sounded far off. But when the lightning struck a tree on the edge off the clearing, causing a giant limb to fall only ten feet from us and completely crushing one of the grave shrubs, I panicked. Pouring raining came out of nowhere, and completely caught me off-guard. In my mind, complete terror broke loose, and I was taken immediately to the place I'd suppressed for so long.

My legs went numb, and I dropped to the ground shaking. I don't know how I'd gone from silent fear to a screaming cry, and my hands covering my ears. All that kept me from having a full-on panic attack was Will. He realized the severity of what was happening, but before he could soothe me the way he wanted, he needed to get us to safety: away from the wind that had picked up, and the possibility of more branches falling. He helped me to my feet somehow (even though they'd all but gone to jelly) and guided me with both of his hands on my shoulders and covering my back with his own body, to a place that looked safe enough to ride out the storm. The way the clouds moved, and his insight to this unique place, told him it'd soon pass. In the interim, he'd have to keep me from succumbing to my panic attack. We sat down and with his arms around me protectively, he sheltered me from the storm.

"Look at me," he spoke loudly enough to talk over the rain. It wasn't coming down with the intensity that had surrounded my parents when they were taken, but it was loud and uniform enough that it caused a yelling whisper to break free of each pine needle above, like a hissing waterfall pouring from the canopy.

I managed to lift my head, and he took my face to hold it and look deep into my eyes. He shook his head up and down as if to say it would be okay, and it was. As he'd predicted in his mind, the quick storm moved out as fast as it'd moved in. If not for the last dripping raindrops coming from the trees up above, it'd have been silent. The air was refreshing, and he hoped it'd help clear my mind. The crickets and tree frogs came back to life, and the feeling returned to my legs.

"Take a deep breath," he spoke calmly, and assuring. "It's okay. You're okay."

At this comment, I fell forward, and just buried my face into his chest and cried. He knew what had just happened. Then and there, he made it his mission to bring me back completely to the person I once was and take all fear from my soul. He wanted to let me live again, and he'd do it with every bone in his body if that's what it took. He was saving me, bit by bit, and I leaned in heavily to somehow transfer from my body to his, a soulful and silent thank you. He really was nothing short of a man. He knew how to be brave and to care for others. He was strong mentally and physically, and he would be my bones when I would feel like collapsing.

It was a while before the rain completely stopped, but once the sound of any water had all but faded, we stood slowly as he helped me to my feet again. He put one arm around my shoulder from the back and the other hand on my shoulder across the front and led me back toward any trail we could find. We were lucky enough to have gotten back on the right one. The grave site and rooster became insignificant, and all we wanted to do was get back home to a place of comfort and familiarity.

As we neared our regular road, we saw lights coming through the woods. Narby, Will's dad, Mr. Leeds, and Randy had all assembled to search for us with flashlights, and we headed toward their voices and silhouettes.

Once in contact, no scolding was handed out. Hugs of relief were all that were given, and even Will accepted a pat on the back from Randy—seeming to let him know he'd done well by caring for me, and also to relay that he'd been worried about his young friend, too. Mr. Leeds and Randy eventually wandered off without even having said a word, and we were left with our guardians.

Everyone remained silent, and Will remained stuck to me like glue in a show of comfort and pure protection. Narby and his dad saw this, but they eventually separated us gently, and led us in opposite directions to our own homes. It was late, and we needed warm showers, dry clothes, and rest. Narby knew exactly what had happened. She only wished she'd known there would be storms that night, as she'd never have let us go. For this, she felt guilty.

An hour later, I'd gotten that warm shower and even a cup of hot tea. Narby asked if I wanted her to stay in my room when I was ready to go to bed and sit in the rocking chair while I slept. I felt better, and exhausted, and just shook my head "No." I would be okay. She kissed my forehead, and left the door open, just a crack.

My room felt a bit muggy from the earlier rains that had kept the windows closed, so I cracked my window to let in the [now bright] moon light and cool air. It felt good and I took a deep breath. Will was right. The fresh air helped to ease tension when I took deep breaths. Though the earlier emotions were terrifying, they were freeing too. Somehow, I grew up a little more with that moment, and Will helped me move forward and face demons I wouldn't have been able to alone.

As I was about to turn from the window, something at the edge of the orchard caught my eye. I turned around quickly to grab my flashlight I'd been toting around like a lifeline the entire night and had put on my nightstand. By the time I got back to the window, I faintly saw two glowing red eyes disappearing into the woods. Fiddling with my light, I finally got it on, and I shined it out as far as it could reach. All I could make out was a man with overalls and a white shirt. The figure nodded at me, as if to say, "*You are safe*", and then vanished.

I wanted to be scared. But instead, I felt I was being protected. Not just by Will anymore, but this entire town that had become home. Everyone here was looking out for me... even the Jersey Devil.

Chapter 8:

A SALTY HOMECOMING

Perhaps my vision of the Jersey Devil had been a hallucination on the tail end of trauma, but my friendship with Will was very real and grew even stronger in the following years. The summer right before high school and when I would turn fifteen, I began to work on the farm alongside him. He taught me much, and I was grateful. He was a farm boy through and through, and he was humbled by it and satisfied with it too. His family was part of the land and town, and, just like the owners of the farm, his roots were deep there, stemming back generations. He was helping me grow my own roots too: caring for me like a new tree and tending to it to make it strong. I had learned of his profound connection to the place here over the years of wandering the woods with him and sharing every last bit possible, of each other's lives. And just like he spoke so highly of the farmers, they spoke the same about him. He was part of the farm just as much as the family who owned it. He was part of its history too. How could he not be? Every person and place he touched was better because of him.

That summer, as I'd pick flowers with one of the farm ladies in the field to sell at the shop or help with the berry picking, his dad would often drive by on a tractor and wave. I'd wave back and then look over toward an adjoining field to see Will smiling at all of us: happy that his blood family, his farm family, and I had all become close. He never failed to show his love for teaching me new things either. I think he was most delighted by teaching me how to assemble corn crates. It was another moment of puffing pride that I recognized from our earlier years of friendship—that I still found endearing even all these years later.

"I still hold the record for most crates put together in under a minute, ya know," he boasted lightheartedly.

I couldn't help but smile, laugh, and shake my head. Here he was, my silly Will, still always trying to impress me any chance he had. By this time, his trying to hide affection for me was almost too much for him to bear, and I often caught him in moments he embarrassed himself. Like one day in the greenhouse for example…

Often in preparation of the winter flower sale, I spent time in the greenhouse planting tiny poinsettia sprouts. Months and months before Christmas, the structure would be hot under the sun, and we'd work away to plant rows—hundreds of pots of flowers—that would become the bright red symbol of the holiday season ahead. Combined with the humidity, it was a sauna in there, and I was usually covered in dirt up to my elbows. I never realized how sweaty I got in there as well. Will walked in one day in the midst of my planting. The two of us were alone, and he'd come in just to say hi in passing, as he always did. When we made eyes, I smiled and waited for a moment for him to say his normal greeting in return, but he looked frozen and wide-eyed. I didn't quite recognize the look in his eyes, but he just stared at me, unmoving. My smile faded partially, and a look of curiosity overcame my face with a questioning furrow. At this, he realized he'd been caught in an act of foolishness [though I still didn't know quite what had gone through his mind], and, after never even saying hello, he left the greenhouse as quickly as he'd entered. I was perplexed but laughed it off as one of the quirks of his I'd come to adore over the years. No matter what came from his mouth, or the actions he showed, I knew they all stemmed from a place of kindheartedness.

When not working at the farm, I was helping alongside Narby on her own property. We had really spruced the place up. In fact, over the years and once I'd seemed to come around out of the dark place after my loss, we'd gotten it back to its original splendor after all. Will helped too, of course, when he had extra time. We painted fences around the house back to their original bright white and used the extra paint to touch up the house where the paint had worn off. We cleared out weeds and mowed fields, pruned the fruit trees (which I'd learned were originally gifted by Farmer Russ's ancestors), and we enjoyed every bit of the hard work together. But no work on either farm kept us away from each other, or from continuing our walks and adventures in the woods. We went on long strolls in the fields too, and plenty of trips to the waterhole as usual and warm evenings talking about future plans were spent under the willow. Although young, we really were both old souls: always seizing the moment and realizing life was too short. He had known this the second I'd told him about my parents, and from that moment we put every effort into making our time together spent to the highest quality of life, if even in our small and humble farming town. We talked about future dreams, and he spoke of wanting to be a pilot. (I understood then why he'd always stopped to watch the crop dusters fly over when we had been younger.) He was infatuated with flight, and it made his eyes light up when he spoke about it. I, on the other hand, wanted to be a writer. Narby had given me a journal as a birthday gift in the past, and since, I'd kept a daily log of my time spent in the Pines, especially with Will.

High school would start for me at the beginning of autumn, and we'd be in different schools. We both knew it, but didn't talk about it much. The blow of reality would come soon enough, and we didn't want to waste this summer thinking about being apart. But something Will often thought about was a surprise he'd kept in the back of his mind for so many years: to take me back to the island to help me overcome my PTSD completely. What he'd seen in the woods year ago touched him so deeply that he'd made it his mission then and there to save me. I was clueless.

I'm not sure when it had come to fruition Narby agreeing to Will's plan to put my pain in the past and go back to the island. But he wanted me to go into my freshman year, feeling just that: fresh. It would be a new start, or at least he'd hoped. Not only that; he wanted me to share with him my home and memories that had come before him, just like he had with me about his own life and hometown so many times since the moment we'd met. I'd spoken of the island of course, but he wanted to be there in person and for me to show him what I felt was important. I knew this, and at the very least, I owed this to him. And so, when they asked me about going back, I let down my guard and agreed. I was nervous, and excited all at the same time; mostly, I was grateful and felt so fortunate for someone to care about me that much. To cross the bridge would mean looking out over the bay to where the marina was. I wasn't sure if I could handle another round of panic, especially since the last time in the woods years ago had been so rough. It'd been a long time since that terror, but it had been so horrifying that it still lingered, and so, I'd learned to cope by burying my feelings. It was no way to live, and not healthy, but it was all that kept me from another meltdown. It seemed nowadays there was just no more room for those memories, so I tried to fill them with anything else, like working hard or wandering with Will. But this time, Narby and Will wanted me to remember the past without anxiety, enjoy the moment I'd be there again, and be able to move forward with no more fear. They realized I buried things, and they wanted me to finally let go of pain, and move on with nothing but positivity, like the little girl I once was.

Almost exactly five years ago, the storm had taken my parents. As it got closer to the time we'd pack up the old blue truck and head east to the island, I did get nervous because of this memory. But Will was with me every step of the way: even reminiscing about the only time he remembered going to the island around age three or four. He remembered the sound of the ocean and the smell of the air, but for some reason, eating sugary cereal in a bay window on an ocean-side rental above a barber's shop was what stuck out the most. And he had come prepared. For the ride down, he figured we'd need a snack. He brought a box of that very cereal and would occasionally crunch like a famished beast just to get a smile from me and take away my apparent tenseness. His cheeriness was so comforting, and his constant yet nonchalant demeanor made for a ride that settled me, and allowed for a softness in the air that would have otherwise made my stomach turn.

It was nice to be back in the truck again. Since we'd moved, we mostly walked everywhere and hadn't taken it out for many trips. But it was a positive and nostalgic change, and hopefully a precursor to what would lie ahead. The bed of the truck was stocked with a few beach chairs, an umbrella, some towels, a cooler with drinks and food, and even some lawn games in another bag. But most importantly, we'd packed an old surfboard that my dad and I had often taken out at sunrise when the break was good, and the working day hadn't quite yet begun. Narby had stored it in one of the barn rafters on the farm, hoping to bring it out again once it was time. It was time. This whole trip was time, and it needed to happen.

In the cabin of the truck sat Narby at the wheel, Will in the middle, and me on the passenger side so I could feel a little less claustrophobic if it came to panic, and be able to roll down the window for fresh air. Just like the night when we were young, when the storm in the woods blew away, the air felt fresh and smelled of pine on this day. Even in August—a typically hot month—it was just a beautiful day with bright blue sky, a few puffy white clouds, and air that felt warm on the skin, but never too hot because of the soothing breeze.

Driving through the forest was a nice hour's ride. We'd only pass through one other little town, more "forgotten" that our own, and the people there were just as kind. A pretty lady with a nice smile and shining eyes waved happily from her hot dog stand when we drove by, and another woman sat just diagonally from the food stand on a large porch of a beautiful old Victorian type home, rocking in a chair and waving as well. Their friendliness wasn't from boredom but from authenticity to be kind to others. I loved that about this place of the pines we had lived for half a decade now—how people were just so unassuming and kind-hearted. I couldn't believe that five years had passed between when we'd left the island, and this very moment when we were heading back to it. It was a happy ride, with Will cracking jokes here and there, and Narby sharing some old stories of my childhood with him while I listened. I think their candid chatter was more to keep my mind busy and from wandering to the point of worry and changing my mind, wanting to turn back.

As we came closer to the island, only a few miles from the water now but still in dense forest, the scent of the breeze began to take change. Intertwined with the pines, was the smell of what my DNA was made of: saltwater. It was unmistakable. Narby could tell I smelled it, too. Will didn't understand the silent words between us on either side of him, but the smell was intoxicating—even for him. The first deep breath, with my eyes closed, took me to my earliest childhood memories, as far back as I can remember: running on the beach with no one around, looking out over a blueish green sea with a clarity most wouldn't expect from waters of the coast of New Jersey, and spinning wildly with my face turned up toward the sun and arms stretched as far as my fingertips would reach. Sea mist would come sporadically with each crashing wave, and the kneading of the wet sand by the water's edge held my feet steady no matter how fast I twirled. These images that seemed ancient now flooded my head and became present again. As I looked out to the right through the window, I grinned with one side of my mouth remembering them.

The landscape faded from the tall Virginia pines to the shorter Pygmy pines. These were all that separated the water from the forest now, so it was only a short matter of time before I saw the marshes.

I put the window down fully to take in the air and release some of my anticipation. Will could sense it, and not knowing if that was good or bad, he nudged his leg on mine. I looked back at him and smiled. It eased his worry and made him smile too. *This was good*, he thought. He was happy his plan seemed to be working out so far.

I looked back out the window, and my first connector to the island came from the sky: a seagull. Higher than most people could see it glided with a high-altitude wind, being carried over the bay below, which I couldn't yet see. Wings straight out to the side, and a white underbelly that was the only way to differentiate him from the sky, he floated with an unseen air current. The closer we got, the bird came down from the sky, low enough to let me hear its call. As if to say, "You're getting closer." There was no holding back now. My smile was beaming, and I felt for Will's hand. He took mine right back, then I looked over at Narby to smile, relieving them both of any worry that this would all go awry.

The pine scrub finally gave way to the marshland, and the first signs of water came in the form of little tidal paths carved through the marsh grass in the back bays, much like the trails through the pines back home. *Home.* It occurred to me at that moment that I was a lucky girl to have two places to call home, two places that held so many good memories, and two places that somehow resembled each other so intimately. Each place kept me grounded, and somehow still tied to the other.

Not only did I now feel my own excitement fully, but I could also sense Will's. Narby had been back on island plenty of times since moving, to visit old friends and check on *Piney Power* (which she kept at a different marina these days after it'd been in an old boat house on the farm for a bit), but Will was excited for his return as well. It had been well over a decade that he'd been on island, so his memories of this place, *my* place, were so few, and I could tell he was chomping at the bits to see if he could remember anything, or just prepare for whatever it was I was willing to share with him. He held back though. He didn't talk. He wanted this to be my day.

The second I made eyes on the bay, I felt myself lean back in the truck a bit as it started up the bridge. The air dropped a few degrees and blew through the cabin—whipping my hair into frenzy and making me close my eyes. It was a beautiful summer day to be out, and, luckily, a weekday which meant fewer tourists. The "weekend warriors" (as we had so secretly referred to them growing up) wouldn't be around yet, nor would it be dead mid-winter and desolate. It'd be a perfect time to bring Will into what was once my only world. I wanted him to be immersed in it with me. I wanted him to feel the ocean on his skin and later what it felt like when it'd dry and leave a salty little prickly feeling behind. I wondered what his eyes would look like when he heard the calling of the gulls, and, if we were lucky, the sighting of a dolphin pod or pelicans. When I looked out over the water as we topped the bridge, sailboats were scattered here and there: a few underway, and a few anchored. I wondered how he'd like to be on the water as I always had.

But beyond the boats, a more familiar sight came into view: the marina. Nothing had changed from what I could see, and nothing had prepared me for this. As small and as far off as they were, I saw the crabbing boats. It was only momentary that I lost my smile and gulped. Perhaps my stomach even twisted a bit, but at the same moment, there was a break in a big puffy white cloud that had temporarily hidden the sun, and a beautiful beam of sunlight came down from high above, and shone straight down on the docks at the marina. And just like that night of shooting stars years ago when I laid by Will's side in a fallow field, I smiled.

That was for me. This was my welcome home.

Chapter 9:

THE MERMAID RETURNS—PART 1

The second one starts descending from the bridge onto the island, every nautical thing the mind can possibly absorb is right there all around you: little shops and houses, the view of the lighthouse if you look north, the clammers in their waders in the mudflats' low tide, boats pulling up crab traps, and docks darting randomly out into the bay like the black keys on a piano with flags flying from the end of each one. On a day with blue sky, a few clouds, a mild temperature, and a slight breeze from the east, it was a perfect homecoming, for sure.

When hitting the crunchy streets for the first time, the feeling of the crushed clams rattled up through the truck tires, throughout the vehicle, and into our bodies. Had Will not been next to me, perhaps I'd have been a bit jarred, but I felt content. Just as he'd guided me by way of fingertip when I'd first arrived in his town—pointing around the pinelands and explaining in detail all of the animals, plants, and places—I now took the lead, and wanted to teach him about mine. As we passed through the island, intentionally in a slow fashion by Narby, I had time to tell the background and stories from my childhood. We waved to some old neighbors and friends who recognized the truck and Narby, and they could see I was an older version of the little girl I'd been than when we'd left here. Rather than looks of shock on their faces to see me having returned, their smiles gave way to happy eyes and looks of joy and relief—that finally I'd been brave and collected enough to return home. I wish they could understand that it was just a visit though, because now my heart had two homes: one connected through the person driving the truck we sat in, and the other whose shoulder brushed mine in a show of support and maybe even something more. Will and I *still* hadn't said anything out loud yet as per our feelings, even after all these years. We didn't have to. I couldn't think of another set of people with a more unspoken and stronger bond than us. He was my other half in a sense, and I wanted to share with him my other half of a place I once called home.

The first place the truck stopped was at the marina. *Piney Power* was there in all her shiny glory, moored at the dock of an old friend's marina. Some friends knew we were coming, so they had polished her up nicely for us. Will finally had a chance to get close to the boat, enough to appreciate the splendor of her lines, curves, and decks. The only other time he'd seen her was years ago when we'd first pulled up coming from the island, with a friend behind us towing her without the mast. That's not a very good impression of such a beautiful piece of craftsmanship. But now, he could see her with the sail and ropes attached, the mast up, and the shiny teak bobbing gently in the water. His love for planes was like mine for sailboats.

Narby asked delicately if I'd like to go for a sail with Will. She wasn't sure if I needed some gentle guiding to ease me back into the feel of the island, or if I was ready to take Will under my wing this time and show him on my own terms, and with my own strength.

"I think I'd actually like to show Will the rest of the place first. Maybe later," I said, feeling confident.

"Suit yourself. She misses you," referring to *Piney Power* and then climbed aboard.

A few friends came down the dock to say hi to us and then followed her aboard as well. Narby noticed that we were standing there trying to figure out who'd drive us around now. She then fiddled in her pocket for a second and pulled the truck keys back out. She tossed them my way. "You know how to drive, Kate. I know Will has been teaching you around the farm in Randy's old truck since he left for college. Just meet me back here at sunset," she said and winked.

I raised my eyebrows, a bit bewildered and with my hand still out in front of me holding the keys. But I turned to Will, smiled, shrugged my shoulders, and we walked back to the truck. We waved to Narby, and they waved back, then undoing the lines so they could motor out to deeper water before raising sail and getting underway.

I turned to Will once we'd watched them head out of the marina, "I know it was a long ride to get here, but I promise you, everything is so close on island, so we'll have plenty of places to get out and stretch."

He just stood there, in front of the truck, smiling at me. "You know I didn't think of it for a second, right?"

"Huh?" I was confused.

"Whether I'm in the car with you for an hour, or five seconds, I don't mind. And I like it," he said, staring into my eyes, like he always had, and just smiled.

I smiled back at him, and he opened the driver door for me. *Gentleman cowboy.*

"Thank you," I said genuinely and directly. At this point, it never ceased to amaze me that such a young person could be such a gentleman. *One-of-a-kind Will.*

Once my door was shut, he hopped in the passenger seat, and shut the door. Then, he just folded his hands in his lap and looked at me as if to ask, "Okay, I'm all yours. Where to?"

I stared at the wheel for a moment and then smiled to myself.

I turned to him then and asked, "Did you ever go surfing?"

"Oh, good grief. You really wanna see me fall?"

Delighted by the thought that I might have actually found something I could do better than him, I didn't miss a beat to reply, "Yep. You drive tractors, I sail boats. You dance, I surf. You in, or not?" I made it sound poetic and playfully taunting, of course.

He smiled. That was answer enough.

August on the island meant warmth: air, sand, and water alike. Summer had been around for a while by this month, and the sea had a good long time to come to a temperature that felt good; the sand seemed to stay at a constant low heat and even the air didn't drop below seventy degrees, no matter day or night. Today was one of those days that all three seemed to coordinate. It made temperature seem to become one with your own body, so that you became one with the island itself. I knew the perfect beach to help Will understand this theory, and so I decided to head toward the north end.

En route, he was enamored by the old captains' homes, and how many hydrangeas could be packed onto one little island. They seemed to blossom everywhere in all shades of pinks, purples, and blues. The gulls stood on rooftops and flagpoles. As I told him the story of the clam-dropping alarm clocks, a gull promptly dropped his own "present" on our windshield. We just stared at it, and then I shook my head smiling when Will commented, "Thank you for that, sir."

Only one main street (just like my new home) was the island's route, with a bunch of smaller streets branching out. Another reminder of how similar my homes were. There were no cars around, as I'd hoped and anticipated. The weekenders weren't around yet, so many of the homes were vacant midweek. I pulled up and parked in front of an old friend's house, and it seemed it was only us.

We cleaned the bird droppings from the windshield, gathered a few towels and the surfboard, and I stuffed a bunch of food and iced sun tea in a bag I'd brought from home; then, we headed toward the beach. The thought of being the only ones around proved true when we made it to the top of the dune walk. As we stood there, I let Will stand in front of me to look out over the sea from the high vantage point. Not another human being was on the beach or in the water. The east breeze was gentle; the seagulls glided in slow motion and seemed to hang on to the wind to keep from racing to the end of the day. These never-ending beach days were what I lived for as a kid. I remembered a handful of them when Narby would take me to the beach for hours at a time when the weather was perfect, so I could play in the sand or in the water. And just as I'd learned to sail, I knew how to surf, too. When I was old enough to swim well, I could paddle out on my own, but not too far. Some days brought these perfectly calm waves, which seemed to break peacefully from one end of the beach to the other. It felt like a forever ride when I could catch one of those swells. Other days, I'd be lucky if I caught only a few waves. But those days were perfect just the same. Just to lie on my board and caress the top of the sea with the pads of my fingers dipping in, being surrounded by the open ocean, and seeing the land from another view, was harmony—pure bliss. Every now and then, the water would have a ripple effect, maybe from a boat that'd passed by far offshore and left a wake, and it'd slap on my board's edge enough to make a little splash in my face over and over. I never knew why my tongue was always first to wipe my mouth before my hands, but I liked the salty taste. I wanted Will to feel this, and to understand what this freedom felt like. My being out in the water, whether on the boat or the board, was the same as him driving the tractor through an endless field or wandering the woods for miles. These were our freedoms. He had shared his with me, and now I would share mine with him.

Once Will took some deep breaths of the sea air that hit him all at once as he topped the dunes, he nodded—as if approvingly—and made his way down the other side toward the ocean with the surfboard. Halfway between the dunes and the shoreline, he stepped on a broken clam shell: not enough to cut himself but it sure felt as if it had. I knew the feeling from so many years of having done the same. I had gotten used to the quick pain, but this was new and momentarily shocking to Will.

"Ah!" he dramatically grabbed his foot. I wasn't sure if he was over-exaggerating or truly in pain. I just watched for a moment, then asked, "You okay?"

He laughed it off, and then picked up the little piece that'd hurt him.

"Your seagull friends planted this I tell you," he alluded of the conspiracy.

"If you can't walk on land, there's no way you're going to stand on the water," I commented as I laughed. He was still game for the trial though and looked at me squinting.

"Yeah? I got this." He laid the board gingerly on the sand, and I put the towels and bag down. He took off his shirt, and I had to look away for a moment. The times at the watering hole when we'd just tossed our clothes onto the ground and gone for a swim, I never spent much time looking at his body. But now, his muscles were standing there right in front of me, not hidden in any shade from pines or dark water. Only, there was no waterhole to jump in to avoid my staring (or lack thereof since I was trying to hide it.) But the reciprocation came when I was left to undress as well. I'd worn a two-piece, and it was the first he'd ever seen me in one. He had no shame, and no reason to look away. And just like when he'd told me awkwardly and out of the blue that I was pretty that one day so many years ago, he looked me dead in the eyes, and I kept my eyes focused on his own while he took a deep breath. But this time, he didn't run. He made it very clear with his staring what he wanted me to know. That explained it all. We had just seen each other in yet another new light.

"So, gonna teach me?" he said, offering me his hand with his back to the water, luring me in playfully, with my surfboard still in the sand.

I picked up my board, "It's not really a matter of teaching." I kept talking, and started walking right past him, and out into the water. I didn't want to break my cool composure and let on to just how desperate I was to feel the ocean on my skin. As soon as I did, it was everything I hoped it would be: cool and warm all at the same time, salt mist in my face, and the sounds of the waves washing around my legs. *Welcome home.*

I plopped the board down gently next to me when the water reached my thighs, laid on it, and looked back over my shoulder. My sandy blonde hair blew gently over my neck and face, getting a little wavier with the salt air as it always had. When I made eye contact with Will, he had that same look on his face as in the greenhouse. Dumbfounded, this handsome boy, with a tan only on his face and lower arms from always only wearing a t-shirt on the farm, just stood there watching me. I didn't know if he was digesting a girl he'd watched grow into a teenager or the fact that he saw me in my element. Whatever his expression, I took advantage of the moment to nod inwardly to get him in the water. He forced himself to stop staring, but I kept watching him as he walked forward. He made it out to stand next to me as I sat up on the board, and he looked at me and smiled. He had no idea he was cute, but as the ocean dripped down his chest and fit stomach, the cute turned into downright handsome. *Randy had nothing on this guy.* Will was good-looking in a simple way, and yet very handsome. There was no mistaking it.

He started walking out in the water again, and as a gentle swell came up and brushed near his ribs, his arms shot up in the air like a proboscis monkey wading in a river. I about fell off my board laughing, and all romance was lost for the moment. He turned back just long enough to smile, send a handful of water my direction, and fell back. When he resurfaced, he just floated. There was no gasp from him, as I'd done when I'd first dove into the bog iron waters in the pines. This water was clear, warm, and moved up and down, not pushing you in any direction like those streams. It made you one with it. Surfing was one step further, and I'd never been so ready to get back up. As he floated around, I laid back down and started paddling. Some of the sticky coconut-smelling wax kept me centered. It'd been years since I was out on the water, and I couldn't wait to catch my first wave. I paddled out beyond Will, but I felt safer knowing he was watching, and he was. He always was.

I saw a few good swells coming, but the last behind a series of four was the one that really caught my eye. I turned the board back toward land and started paddling. As soon as I felt the familiar nudge from the sea telling me to stand, I did. My sea legs were back, and I didn't falter. Just ten seconds of a ride and nothing fancy, but when I flopped backward off the board into the water, I was smiling. Will was in awe. I paddled back out near him again.

"That was incredible! How did you remember how to do that after so long? You looked… flawless." There was a double edge to that comment, but I pretended not to hear. I wanted to stay in my salt world and my salt world only, at least for the time being.

I replied taunting a bit like he once had with all his fancy dancing I was clueless about, "Like I said it's not a learned thing. You either feel it or you don't. I can't teach you really. You'll just have to show me what ya got," I said and winked.

With that, he took the hint. As we stood on either side of the board, he pulled it gingerly in his direction signaling for me to hand it over. That I did. I stayed where I was, rather than swim back to shore, just in case it really did turn into a disaster. Off he went, back out to where it became waist-deep, and tried to mimic my every move from earlier. I was quite impressed seeing such a rugged and muscular young man, paddling softly in his own style, out into the deep blue. Like Will had felt when I became connected to his land, he was now connected to my water. It was a sense of delight and deep satisfaction all at once that made me sigh. I was happy, just plain happy. And it felt good. In my element, I stood surrounded by sounds and smells, that I'd almost lost or buried, watching someone I loved so much enjoy a place I loved so much. The world stood still when we played in it, and it was he who'd brought me back. *Wait, I loved Will? I mean, yes. Of course, I did. But I'd said it in my mind!*

Time and time again, he'd stand and then fall. Relentlessly, he just kept trying. It was amusing beyond belief, especially to see him slap the water with his hand extra dramatically each time he flopped. I felt comfortable enough to watch from the beach since he was a strong swimmer, so once back on the shoreline, I sat and let my legs lay flat pointing out in his direction with my toes in the water, and just propped myself up on my elbows. After a few more flops on his end, I felt bad. He'd taught me so many things, so it was my turn to teach him.

I yelled out sarcastically to where he was in a manner of being forced to do so, "Okay, Okay. I'll give you some pointers. It's very clear you're a guy in need of help."

"Alright, but the teacher is only as good as what the student learns. If I fail, that's on your shoulders," he shouted back.

I swam out, once again feeling welcome and at ease in my happy place. When I had made it to him, I felt funny saying to someone bigger than me, "I'll hold the board still. You just lay down, and I'll push you when the wave comes."

That I did, but I was already under a wave on the back part of the board when it started to roll over me and it created quite the sight: Will sitting like a toad on the front, me on the back hanging on, and my legs trailing out behind. We just laughed like fools, spitting out water on the easy wave 'til the ride was over.

We kept laughing and laughing. Then I finally said, "We must have looked ridiculous!"

"To whom?" he asked, becoming a little less comical, and reminding us both that we were alone, on [what felt like] a deserted island, with an entire beach and space of ocean to ourselves. This knowledge being felt, I pushed the board far enough that it washed up back to shore itself, and we were left, wading up to our knees again under the bright sun and above the twinkling sea shooting light up from below. It appeared the reverse of when the sunshine shown down through the pine needles in the woods, and I think he was catching on of this semblance between the two places. I could feel him enjoying his time here, and there was so much more I wanted to show him.

We waded around a short while longer and then headed back to the beach for a snack. We sat down to share one towel, so we could save the other as a dry spare. Narby had packed us some peanut butter and jelly sandwiches, potato chips, and sun tea, and I'd grabbed a few to put in my beach bag to carry more easily to the beach. She made the sun tea herself and she must have taken pointers from Will as to proper storage since it was still so cold and refreshing in the little containers she'd poured it in.

"Man, this is chilly tea!" he said.

"I was just thinking you must have lent her your canteen," I said, and he smiled, finding it cute that I remembered his childhood thermos. Then, his smile turned to a look of intrigue and slight disgust as I dissected my sandwich, separating each side and stuffing the chips into the middle.

"Oh, just try it. C'mon," I gave him a nudge.

"Fine. Gimme a chip, ma'am," he said and held out his hand.

He put a few of the chips I'd given him in what was left of his lunch and took a bite. A pensive look came over his face and then slowly formed into a smile.

"Hey, you're onto something, kid," he said as he nodded in approval.

"You know I'm older than you, right?" After years and years of his pet name for me, I had to call him out on this endearing commentary.

He was instantaneous with comebacks, "Yeah, but I gotta care for ya like you're mine. My little lady." His cowboy tone had returned a smidge.

"Little, too, eh? You might be taller, but don't forget I'm *older*," I said jokingly and laid down my verbal note and used the older part to my advantage now.

"Okay. *Old* lady. Better?" he smirked as he asked.

"Ha, very funny," I said and nudged him again, and he smiled at me. His eyes were so blue at that moment: deep, ageless, and bright blue. I'm not sure if it was the combination of sea and sky, but they took my breath away. He leaned forward on his side of the blanket looking out to the sea: his elbows on his knees, and his forearms extending out comfortably with one hand gripping the rest of his sandwich.

"Well, with age comes wisdom, right? Common sense and all that, *ooold* lady?" he continued, dragging out the age mention.

At that very moment, a seagull swooped in and stole the rest of his lunch that he wasn't paying attention to.

"Yes. Wisdom," I said and grinned with an extra wide and coy smile.

Chapter 10:

THE MERMAID RETURNS—PART 2

When we'd finished our impromptu beach picnic (or what had been left of it after the sneak attacks by the gulls), we packed the board and our belongings back in the truck and decided to head to the light-house. I thought it was only fair I show him the local landmarks and not just the places of my personal memories.

The lighthouse stood tall and proud, red and white, and—against a blue sky—it was as American as one could get. I always had a sense of hometown pride and patriotism when I stood below her and looked up.

"Wanna go up?" I asked. "Only two-hundred and seventeen steps to the top."

"Well, you might think I'm beat after surfing, but I think I still have some energy left, old woman," he smirked, continuing to rub in his new pet name for me. He had such a way of being charming and willing regardless that he was probably a bit beat and exhausted from surfing for almost a good hour. He started toward the door of the light's base, hunched over like an old-timer using an invisible cane. I rolled my eyes in embarrassment for him, and giggled.

After climbing up the twisted yellow steps of the interior, the top of the lighthouse welcomed us with an endless view—three-hundred and sixty degrees of boats, blue sky, turquoise sea, white sand, and scrubby trails through the green dunes. Somehow, the salt air even made its way to this height, and the breeze continued to freshen up our souls. We sat down beside one another and let our feet dangle through the edge of the iron fence bars, which surrounded the top of the light to keep anyone from falling.

"This is really nice, you know. I mean, thanks for taking me around," he said in a very honest-to-goodness and direct way.

"Thanks for taking me in the first place, Will. This was all your idea," I replied.

"I've been wanting to do this for a while. What happened years ago in the woods... I just... well I never wanted you to feel that way again," he was so authentic.

"Why are you so good to me?" I asked him, just about as straight-forward as he was being.

"Because you're good to me, too. You always have been," he said back, just as unswervingly.

I knew what he meant. He knew what I meant. Since the day we'd become friends, we'd always put each other first. We cared deeply about each other like we'd never cared for anyone else. We were inseparable, best friends, and more.

A familiar sight broke the contemplation between us. *Piney Power* was passing by at that exact moment, and I yelled out, "Narby! Hey! Up here!"

A motorboat would not have heard my call for connection, but now under a soft sail, Narby and her few friends (that had filled in for me and Will as crew), looked up our way and waved, "Ahoy, there!"

The energy of the island was rushing again through my veins and I sprung back to my feet once I got them out between the safety railings of the lighthouse ledge. I looked at Will, "Ready to see more?" I must have looked like an eager puppy. But Will had a different look. Almost like he had been let down.

I asked quickly, "Did I do something wrong?"

After a momentary pause, that I think was unintentional, he spoke, "Oh, gosh, no. Sorry, Katie. Just, the sailboat. She looks so pretty in her element. She's... beautiful."

For some reason, I knew there was more to his compliment than he let on, as usual. He wasn't talking about the boat; he wasn't even looking at the boat. He was staring at me, and I had interrupted a moment for him. He was watching my happiness, and it was assuring him that bringing me here was the best thing he'd ever done for me. But he wasn't about to let anything get in the way of a day that was meant for one thing only: to help me move on, and remember nothing but joy, and no more pain. And for the rest of the day, that's all it was: lawn games on the beach, more swimming, saltwater taffy from a candy store called Harvey's, and some grilled shellfish at our family friends' old clam shack of a restaurant. Visits here and there to more landmarks and running off the end of a dock in the bay that seemed like the dock back home made him feel just as at ease as I was.

Hours later, when the sun began to set, as promised, we headed back to the marina to meet Narby. Having just pulled in from the nice offshore sail we'd seen them heading out for earlier, they all looked refreshingly sea-washed and sun-kissed.

Narby caught my attention while pulling into the slip, "Kate, I decided to stay here on island for the night. We're going to go out for dinner and drinks, and we'd love you and Will to join us if you'd like." She spoke kindly, but also leaving us unsure of what our options were. *How would we get home if we chose not to go to dinner?*

Narby must have seen the look on our faces once again, so she just shook her head and laughed, "Oh, you two. Listen, just take the truck home. It's a peaceful and safe ride, so go enjoy yourselves." Technically, her suggestion was illegal since neither of us were licensed drivers, but I was only a year away from getting mine and we both knew how to drive, probably even more responsibly than most licensed youths. We humbly kept the keys, said our goodbyes, and then went our opposite ways. Will held the door for me once again, but this time, I didn't get in the truck, and handed him the keys instead.

"Your turn. Old ladies don't drive once the sun sets," I smirked.

Going back over the bridge amid a beautiful sunset, was a great farewell and good end to the day. I felt the prickle of dried saltwater on my skin, and by the way Will rubbed at his forearms every now and then, I could tell he felt it too. I could also sense that he got it now and he knew why this place was so dear to me: the people we'd bumped into throughout the day, the colors and brightness of a good beach day, the feeling of the sea, and a different smell in the air than our usual pines. As much as I'd loved my trip back to the island, heading off now felt the true direction of home. I loved the smell of salt air, but the smell of the pines had become a part of me, and my true home. After all, it was the one I shared with Will.

Driving through the great forest with the windows cracked gave way to that very pine scent and relaxed us as though we'd been at a spa all day. Even our feet were softened from having walked on the sand for so long, and our bodies felt like mush from all the swimming and sun. I looked forward to getting back, and maybe just sitting under the willow for a nap, or even an early bedtime. When I spoke the latter out loud, Will wanted no part of it.

"What? Nap? Early bed? And ruin the perfect day?" he said sounding flabbergasted that I'd even suggest cutting short our time spent.

"Ha! Ok then, what did you have in mind, *Old Timer*?"

He found this amusing that I was referring to him as an elder as well, making us on an even playing field.

As we finally pulled onto the sandy road that joined our individual farms, he suggested the waterhole, of course. *How could I say no?*

We found our way down our regular path at a leisurely pace: the whole way reminiscing about the day behind us.

"I get it now. Why you are so attached to the island, that is," he said and smiled endearingly, glad I'd finally and fully let him into my past.

84

"I'm really glad you took me, Will," I said and wrapped my arm in his in a show of gratitude as we strolled side by side.

"What's going to happen next year?" he said and became solemn suddenly, and I felt his arm slump a bit.

"What do you mean?" I replied.

"You're going to high school." Again, he spoke with that ever-wise old-soul of his, realizing our childhood was ending. His sinking heart fell as quickly as the sun and must have been contagious, as I started to feel a bit of longing to hold on to this last summer too—this last bit of innocent youth—as he'd just said it out loud. It hit me like a brick.

"Nothing is going to change. And that's exactly what's going to happen next year to answer your question. Nothing will change," I said it twice, in part to convince him, part wanting to convince myself. But the truth was, I didn't know. I could only hope.

We ended up at the dock by the water as usual and sat down.

While both of us just stared into the brown water, which was illuminated by the rising moon, I giggled a bit, "Hey, remember that day in the greenhouse, when you didn't talk, and just left?"

I could feel his face turn toward mine, so I looked at him too, and listened. His face was serious.

I finished, "What happened? I always wondered about that."

He replied, "A drop of sweat ran down your face—from your forehead, and down the side of your cheek. You were so dirty, and your hair was so messy. You were the most beautiful thing I'd ever seen. You still are."

Had it not been for the frogs starting to chirp in the early evening, he could have heard me swallow. We didn't move. Not a muscle. There was nothing romanticized about this. No exaggerating, nor one of his silly stories trying to make it bigger than it was. This was his pure truth.

My eyes dropped a bit from his, and then I turned my head back toward the water. I tilted my head, placing it on his shoulder, and closed my eyes. He put his arm around me and kissed the top of my forehead for as long as a single kiss would allow.

All he'd done for me that summer and getting me back to the island to move on with life in a positive direction had made me come around. Heck, all he'd done for me since the day I showed up in his little town had made me come back to life. He cared about me from the second we met. Without doubt, we were the loves of each other's lives. We just didn't say it. We didn't need to.

Chapter 11:

FROM COUNTRY ROADS TO COUNTRY STARS

Much to our delight, nothing did change in high school, just as we'd hoped. In fact, almost the entire time went by without much change at all. We worked side by side at the farm, we continued to go to the carnival each year (and I'd finally given in to dancing), and we spent time in the woods and even on the island. Will became a pretty good surfer, and I had started to teach him how to sail as well. I figured it was only fair as he'd taught me how to drive the infamous green tractor. Over the years, we'd spent evenings under the stars talking about future plans. I'd become a good writer: even if starting out writing in the journal, I now wrote columns for our local paper as a low-paying side job as well. Will had become even more fascinated with crop dusting and I knew he was destined for flight. He'd picked up books here and there to study, and his eyes never ceased to light up when a plane went over.

At the start of senior year, I knew I needed to make the most of it. In less than a year, I'd be going to college, and we'd be apart more than ever before. He'd planned a day entirely for me on the island years before, and I had a plan up my sleeve to surprise him as well.

Under the watchful eyes of Mr. Leeds and The Mayor, I took the smaller tractor out into a soybean field late one September night, and turned on its lights. Luckily, it was one of the furthest fields from Will's house. With my talent learning to drive over the years, I'd helped cut corn mazes for the fall festivals at the farm. This time, I'd be cutting some words, and it'd be a bit easier in a lower-growing crop. Nighttime would be the challenge though, so the next morning would be the big reveal if all had been perfectly spelled out. I needed to be patient. After hours of hoping for perfection, Mr. Leeds and his skunk did a thorough investigation and he nodded in approval: sending me off on my way back to my own farm. I'd not seen it yet, but somehow Mr. Leeds used his farm sense and expertise to assure me my work was done right, so off I went. The early morning would come and would be the second part of my plan.

Crop-dusting really is a huge part of farm life. Luckily for me, our local sprayer was close friends with Mr. Leeds, and they'd already discussed taking me up over the field in the morning to make sure my writing had come out in perfection. As we took off from a local runway in a larger plane than the normal spraying plane, the aerial view of the land was an entirely new sense for me. A natural map from the sky, the autumn colors made me feel as though we were flying over a fire. But there was no smoke—only oranges and yellows of fields and forests, not quite ready to turn to the deepest shades of their respective colors yet. The pilot gave me sign that we were coming up on the soy field, and I was anxious with anticipation to see my work. When it came into view, I was delighted. It read: *Prom, Will?*

I was so proud that I clapped my hands in a rapid little motion that could have resembled a squirrel delighting over an acorn. Yes, I was asking a boy to prom. Maybe not so ladylike, but I'd given up on trying to be so over the years. I wasn't as much a tomboy as I'd used to be, but I was steadfast, strong, and determined, and, to me, there was nothing more feminine than going after what you wanted, and my little field message proved so. I had accomplished a great work, and I only hoped Will would find it as satisfying and flattering.

Later that day, as planned, it was Will's turn to go for a plane ride. Mr. Leeds and I told him we'd talked the pilot into taking him up for a lesson to start him in flight school. I drove him to the little airport in the next town, where I'd already been that morning. The pilot was waiting. Will boarded the plane, and off they went. I only wished I could have been there to see him react as he read my crop-carved signage, but when he came back less than twenty minutes later, the look on his face was all I needed. He got off the plane, ran to me, picked me up, and twirled me around.

"Of course!" he shouted.

"Wait; I have more!" I giggled. I told him to close his eyes and hold out his hand.

With his eyes closed, he asked, "It's not a snapping turtle is it?" He laughed.

It was a belt-buckle with a plane on it. A perfect combination of his western wildness and his love for the sky.

"Open your eyes," I said, placing it in his hands, "So, you can always remember this, and that your dreams of flying will come true," I added.

He looked as though he'd get choked up. "Katie. But why? Is this a holiday I don't know about?"

"Will, you opened my eyes to what home really means. I just don't want you to ever forget me when you move on with life and chase your dreams."

His face seemed to drop more each time I spoke throughout my explanation, and eventually he just interrupted me. "First: *you* are the one who will be moving on… in less than a year!"

He'd said it out loud, and it stung.

"Second: whatever dreams come true, you're going to be in them. You are my best friend, my everything. Everything I've become is because you've been by my side," he added.

At that, I couldn't help but tear up a little. It was silent, and a few just rolled down my cheeks. I wiped them away, quickly making short of it since I was so embarrassed. "Oh stop; you're getting me all greenhouse!"

At that, we laughed. There were so many memories between us, and it was inevitable there were more to come. He was right: wherever we went and whatever we did, somehow, it would be together.

Although this was only a school dance (that was still over a half year away), I wanted to make it larger than life for him, as he'd always done with things for me. He'd know just how special he was, and it'd be the perfect ending to high school before I started college. In fact, I'd already applied to a few: some local, and one in New England. I'd always had a fascination with New England, though I'd never been there. The pictures and saltwater lifestyle seemed to call my name. I was planning on going to school for journalism so I could take over the job of editor in our hometown once I graduated. It wouldn't be a high-paying job, but the money wasn't what I wanted. I just wanted to be home for good once school ended, and have a job that kept my mind smart. In the meantime, I hoped to be on the sailing team if I did go north. Maybe even get a scholarship for it. Of course, I'd want Narby and Will to visit as often as possible. It was only five hours north, and heck—if Will got his pilot's license sooner than later, he could fly up to see me anytime! Truth be told, I'd probably stay local. My heart was here, and I didn't want to leave. All these thoughts raced through my mind in a flurry, and I had plenty of reasons convincing me that we'd always stay this close. There was only a small bit of worry since it would be the first time we were truly apart after being together almost every day for the better part of our young life. But really, *what did I have to worry about?*

Senior year flew by, and prom came fast. Had it been years ago, I'd have considered wearing overalls to the dance, but I'd come to know a little fashion at least. Even if it was simple. Dorey was more rugged like me, but she had grown up around money and a fancier lifestyle, and really did understand a good sense of fashion. She gave me tips throughout the year leading up to prom, and even convinced me to wear a long dress… even if it'd be hard to walk in. For this, I felt better prepared. (Narby felt relieved.) Finally, she would see me in something other than jeans and mud!

I ended up back on the island for my dress. Some of the fancy out-of-towners had moved there as Narby had mentioned, and, as it turned out, a few weren't that bad. Narby had befriended a nice woman from the city who decided to retire full-time from her bridal boutique and tough out the winters at the beach. The islanders had bets she wouldn't survive one cold season, but years later they had to eat their words. She was a bit flashier than everyone else, but she also helped everyone. When the going got tough, she was right there to put in her hard work alongside the rest of them, so she was welcomed all the same. She didn't stop working either. Like Narby, they had this in common. She opened a little dress shop just to keep her mind busy, and her hand in the business. It didn't hurt that she was very well-known as a celebrity stylist either. In season, the out-of-towners paid top dollars for her custom designs and it kept her busy. Yacht club parties, white parties, themed dinners, beach dinners. They all needed to be the best of the best, so they came to her shop, and they kept her schedule [and bank account] full. Narby and she really bonded over this hard-working, female, go-get-'em gusto, and I felt honored when she offered to design a prom dress for me—for free!

She had asked me to choose a color a month before prom, and she would do the rest. It was easy for me. I went to the beach, picked a piece of dune grass, and brought it to her. She understood without question. A week before the big night, Narby told me the dressmaker was coming to meet us at the farm. I arrived after a day working on a column at the newspaper, so thank goodness I was clean and not dirty like after a good farm day!

Out from a long, opaque, zippered bag, she pulled the dress. It was the first time Narby or I had seen it. In fact, Narby hadn't even known the color. It matched the sample I'd picked from the beach perfectly. It was a strapless satin gown, cinched a small bit at the low of the back, and falling just below my ankles. A few little starfish made of pearls at the bottom of the hidden zipper in the back were sewn on. I had never worn a long dress before, let alone one that looked like it belonged on a movie star. She'd even brought a pair of shoes to match.

"Now, we all know you do not wear heels, so I had a friend make some sandals. Just think of them as stylish flip flops," she assured me, and winked.

They were comfortable and flat, with a few little starfish to match those on the dress.

Narby was beyond excited. "Well! Go try it on!"

I was so grateful that I was speechless. I took the dress and sandals and headed upstairs. There was a huge, long mirror Narby had convinced Will to bring out of the attic a few weeks ago (though he had no idea why, and didn't ask either, just assuming it was for common use). I found it in one of the many bedrooms, and undressed, just to get dressed again.

Once done zipping up, which I found very easy, surprisingly pleasant, and dainty, I turned to look. I had no expression. I looked from neck to toe, and back again. *Was this really me?* I couldn't believe how perfectly it fit, and how the color seemed to reflect in my eyes. I looked at my eyes then even closer. Face to face with myself, I saw my mother. I remembered a picture of her in her wedding dress. Though her dress was white of course, it was as if I was looking at her. I smiled. The memories of my parents only brought joy these days, and I didn't bury them anymore, thanks to Will.

I walked back down a few sets of old, creaking staircases. When I reentered the living room, the ladies were having some of Narby's tea, and they looked at me and smiled.

"Yep, that's the one," the dressmaker said with pride.

"Oh goodness! You look so pretty, my dear," Narby quickly chimed in. They made some more endearing compliments, and Narby ended the conversation lightheartedly, "Now go take it off before you get it dirty!"

I laughed, remembering who I was, and went to tuck it snuggly away until prom. It was still a week away, but for some reason I had butterflies.

The big day rolled around fast, and it felt like it was just yesterday I was trying on the dress, but here I was, back in front of the mirror, putting it on again. Though this time, I struggled with the zipper. I called for help, and Narby came to the rescue.

After zipping me up, she gave me a little box. "I was saving these for your wedding day, but I just had to give them to you now."

I tilted my head to the side with curiosity, laughing a little that she'd even consider me marrying any time soon, and took the box gently. Opening the box, there were two, small, pearl drop earrings.

"Your mother's. She'd have wanted you to have them. Besides, they match the starfish." I believed she said the last part just to make the first part of the comment less emotional and keep her from showing it.

It was one thing to have seen my reflection resemble her weeks prior, but to be wearing a piece of her almost brought me to tears.

"Oh, Narby. Geez. Thank you," I said and hugged her tightly.

"Alright now, don't get me all teary. Besides, you don't want your make-up to run."

We both laughed heartily knowing I had none on, nor did I have any intention of wearing any. No hairspray, no nail polish, no make-up, no ma'am! Just me. The dressmaker had suggested a few "artists" to complete my look, but the thought of letting people at my face with brushes, pencils, powder, and paint was horrifying. I had politely declined. They had both laughed. They told me I was lucky I'd grown into a beautiful young lady, and didn't need make-up anyway.

"Well, go do whatever else it is you have to do. I'm sure Will is going to be here soon." Then, she stopped in the doorway and spun around. "Wait! I forgot." She reached into her pocket, tossing me something that I caught without faltering. "It's yours. Not to borrow either. Consider it an early graduation present."

I couldn't believe it. She had passed the truck on to me!

"Take care of her," she concluded with a wink, and walked out.

I was left to look at myself again. I had done my hair in a simple low twist, and when putting the earrings on, it all came together. In fact, I was quite pleased with my appearance.

When I was putting the last flip flop on (I refused to call them sandals), I heard the knock at the door. *Will!*

Narby had let him in, and when I came into the room, she left us to be alone. He slowly turned, and became immediately still and silent when he laid eyes on me. I felt it too. I was breathless to look at him. I'd never even imagined him in a suit. His body from years ago at the beach had filled out and his suit fit him perfectly. I was too shy to look at him from head to toe, but I couldn't help but notice he had a pair of shiny black cowboy boots on and the belt buckle I'd given him. You could dress him up, but you couldn't take the country from him! He was handsome. A grown cowboy. *Cowman?* I had no words. In my own head, I couldn't even find my words. He even smelled like a man, too. It gave me a little chill.

From his side, he brought a little bouquet of white flowers to his chest. "You…" He kept staring. Slowly, he held out the flowers as he got closer. I held out my hand to accept them, and when our fingers brushed, we felt something we never felt. It was deep. Very deep. Silent but deep. He whispered then, "You are so beautiful."

I was still and silent. I hadn't said a word yet. I couldn't. Every sense was whirling around in my head, and it took a moment before I could speak. "Thank you," I half choked, half whispered, still trying to absorb the person in front of me.

"I… I have something for you too," I said, regaining my composure, but he still looked in awe.

On his suit jacket, I began to tack a little pin. With my next blabbering explanation, I broke the chemistry between us for the time being. "Mr. Leeds never had a son. He talks about you with so much pride like you are the one he never had. He was a pilot in the war, you know. He never told us this. I mean, he told me. Anyway, we knew you'd feel funny wearing a flower, so he told me to give this to you. This is his flight school graduation pin," I said but I was just rambling now because I was so nervous.

Will looked slowly down my arm to my hand as I delicately attached the pin to him. I was shivering a bit, and my hands were cold—I was so tense. Then, he looked back up my arm just as slowly, to my neck. It was the same face he had on when he saw me in the greenhouse. He spoke so softly, "I don't know what to say. This is perfect. Thank you." He put his hand over mine, over his heart, and held it for a second.

I tried to break the quiet. It wasn't that it bothered me. I just didn't know what to say either. I finally said something, "Look!" I made him hold out his hand and dropped the keys into them.

He chuckled a bit. "So, we get to drive Narby's truck again, huh?"

"No. We get to drive *my* truck," I said and smiled with delight.

"No way! She gave it to you?" He was happy for me.

"Early graduation present, she said. But I want you to drive it."

He understood. I wanted to let him be a man. The man that he was.

We were still just quiet and staring again, until Narby walked back in. "No leaving until I take a picture! Can't have you walking out without at least one, right?"

She insisted that we stand on the porch steps beside some newly blooming flowers. After she took the shot, she hurried us off to "go have some fun" as she always had in the past and then left us to ourselves again.

After she went back inside, he held my hand and walked me to the truck, and then helped me inside. Before he shut my door, he stared at me again for a second. It was the same look from the first time we'd met, when he handed me the flowers. Only this time, I was the one blushing.

Chapter 12:

WHERE THE SANDY ROAD STOPS

When arriving at the dance, the breathlessness between us seemed to have become contagious. People stopped dead in their tracks: staring at us, as if almost to try and recognize the couple who'd gone from country fields, to country stars.

We didn't notice it though. We were still mesmerized by one another and attached at the hand as always. Though, this time, it meant a whole lot more. Not to mention whatever it was between us was very public now. It was all out there in the open that we were together, not just as friends, but as a couple. There was no denying the way Will stared at me with deep passion, and I felt like the center of his universe. Everyone could see it. Kitty could see it. She was more jealous than ever. She wasn't in the spotlight anymore; we were.

There were some friendly hellos, compliments, and kind words by farm kids and the wealthy ones alike. It was a night everyone was equal and there for a good time and an early farewell to many years of being together, so a bit bittersweet as well. Some faster-tuned party songs started off the evening, but I knew what Will and I both were waiting for: something slow so we could hold each other close. And that we did. As soon as the first mellow love song came on, Will held out his hand to lead me gently by the fingertips out to the center of our gym auditorium. It was decorated in a Hollywood theme. Ironically, Kitty was on the board of school event planning, and this was to be her big show and pretend to be a movie star, I supposed. She wanted to be the starlet of her own movie, but there we were, on the makeshift walk of fame, dancing on our own star under soft lights, and holding each other in a way that showed just how connected we were. At this sight and at the entire scene—she was raging mad. She was even more furious when Dorey [I do believe, purposely] let the cat out of the bag with the news of who designed my dress. Kitty was livid. Will and I never saw it though. We never cared to give her the time of day, as this was our night together. This was the first, and maybe last time for a while that we'd dance like this, and she wasn't going to ruin it. But she was scathing. Others saw it. Her friends saw it. But this time, they stepped in. They held her back from stealing the floor and let us have our time together. They'd finally found their own voices over the years and didn't let her control them anymore. Though other couples joined in around us, we owned that night. We savored that moment together. With one of my arms around his neck, one of his around my waist, and our other hands entwined, there was a chemistry that the entire room felt. It was a moment of magic. Our lives together thus far had always been an internal bond, but this was being free, and not being afraid to just be friends anymore. The night continued with song after song, even a few air guitars by Will to make me laugh as always, and I may have even chimed in a bit with an invisible microphone from time to time, especially when one of our favorites came on. As fun as it all was, the night was still young. There was to be the special senior bonfire later. Will wasn't the only underclassman there, and no one discriminated who showed up anyway. It was just some good local fun we Pineys lived for.

One by one, couples departed at the end of the dance, and left the high school for the woods. Most of us changed first in our cars: leaving our fancy clothes behind for jeans, tees, and sweatshirts. Will and I had different western-style boots over the years, but somehow always managed to pick the same color leather. He had on a sweatshirt from the farm, and when I stuck the old green tractor hat on his head that he'd brought along, he took out an extra hoodie to put on me. He'd given me the privacy I needed to slip out of my dress beforehand, or at least I had hoped!

The bonfire had already started when we arrived, as a few other farm boys had left earlier from the dance to get it going. Of course, there was less organization, and more of making a wood pile and lighting it on fire, than the critique of Kitty's prom planning. At least it seemed that way. Truth be told, those boys knew much more about the safety of the woods than anyone in the school, so rightfully it was their job. Anyone else trying to light a fire that big would have surely burned the forest down. Kitty may have done it on purpose just for attention had she been left in charge!

Old, dry stumps were scattered around the fire for seats, and—like many mischievous high schoolers—there was plenty of cheap beer to go 'round, too. Will sat on a stump for two, and I just plopped myself right on his lap giggling. This new "outed relationship" was easy, and we couldn't keep our eyes off one another. There was no more trying to hide the stares or the flirting between us. It felt darn good.

Dorey wandered over at one point, shaking her head, "Oh, you two. We all saw this coming. About time!"

We all laughed together, and she took a seat on a long log next to us with her date. Like her, he came from an affluent farm family, but the old money in him reflected a gentleman farmer. He was polite, sophisticated, and made Dorey feel like a million bucks. She deserved it. She too had traded in her boots for some heels earlier for prom and looked so pretty that night. She even tried out some lipstick, though it had been taken off (along with the heels), on the ride over to the bonfire. Dorey and I got each other: all natural, backwoods girls. No reason to pretend we were something we weren't. We were true to ourselves and that was all that mattered. We had nice conversation between us, and Dorey and her date shared a beer. We'd all had a beer or two over the years, but, as always, didn't make a big deal about it, nor do it to get drunk. A crew of old souls just enjoying a beverage after long days was all it had ever amounted to. We preferred the sweet tea anyway. Our crew was comprised of those accustomed to being up early mornings and working hard. We didn't have the luxury of sleeping off a hangover like Kitty and her fancy gal pals.

A few crates had been donated by parents, and filled by all of us with sticks, marshmallows, hot dogs, and rolls. It really was a good ol' country time back there, and a nice connecting piece of our souls before most of us would all go separate ways at the end of the coming summer. Most of the farmers would likely end up back home, but the rest were unknowing of where they'd end up. Maybe a few would move forever, as some had a downright plan to escape our little town. But Will had a plan to come back to become the local crop duster, and I knew the editor position at the paper would be waiting for me. We had no desire to run from a good life and were grateful to be sitting with each other to reminisce about it.

Kitty arrived, fashionably late (and still seething) of course, but no one cared anymore. No one was afraid anymore. Everyone had grown up and found their own solid ground. The loud sounds of guitar music and chatter drowned out her negative energy anyway. Even though she had a sweet smile on her face, many of us recognized the underlying evil that had remained in her veins since childhood and knew her expression was all fake. I'd say I never truly met a bad person in my life, but most sitting around the fire that night would agree with me: Kitty had hate in her soul. We just refused to let it get under our skin anymore.

She walked right over toward Will and me, and we prepared for the worst. Though we had no fear of her, we didn't want this precious time together to be spoiled either. Dorey rolled her eyes, and her date excused himself to grab another drink. He supposed if he was going to sit through a lecture, he may as well be prepared.

"You know, this has been a long time coming," she stated, primly and properly as always. *(We braced ourselves.)* "I owe all of you an apology."

If the guitars a few folks had brought to play had been accompanied by a record, you'd have heard it halt to a screeching stop. Everyone stopped and quieted and—regardless if in conversations of their own—they were all tuned into ours now. Kitty reveled in knowing she'd gotten the spotlight back.

Turning to everyone now, which was just about our entire class, she continued, "Actually, I owe everyone an apology." It was the biggest load of garbage we'd ever heard come out of her mouth. Dorey walked away. It was unlike her to have little manners, but she'd had enough. After more than a decade of being the victim of Kitty's assaults, and she wasn't about to give her an ounce of attention. But it didn't hinder Kitty one bit, and everyone else listened intently: more for entertainment than true interest.

"Over the years, I've been brash. I know. But sometimes, we must hold our heads high to move forward," Kitty waved her head around, batting her eyes, as if too good for the company around her.

No one had any clue what she was talking about.

She turned directly to Will and transformed her cat face into that of a sweet kitten. It was her greatest performance yet. "Anyway, I know I've been hardest on you. Will, I am so very sorry for having always picked on you. Really, I always thought of you as a great dancer, and I sure do like those new boots."

Everyone shook their heads at Kitty, only to reassure each other that no one was buying what she was selling. Now, I was the one seething. She knew those words got to me, and she loved it. For four years, she'd not bothered us much at all. Other than a snide glare in a hallway from time to time, she really had seemed to grow up a bit. But this was a low blow. It wasn't directed at Will either. It was thrown straight at me. She was flirting with him right in front of me. Will seemed to falter for a minute, trying to search in his mind for a reply. And when he did, it was simple.

"Thank you," he spoke non-poignantly with no respect nor kindness in his face, but more so to say: *I acknowledge it, and now we can move on?*

Perhaps no one else could see it as her back was now turned to the rest of the crowd, but I could sense it in the air, that his reply was not what she was looking for. So, she made a very bold move. She held out her hand and asked him to take a walk! "Grab a drink with me and let's start fresh?" she asked him.

Everyone looked at him now with shocked expressions, wondering what he'd do. She reassured him that she just wanted to go grab a drink, give him a toast, and tell him one-on-one that she was genuinely sorry. He looked at me, making sure I knew going with her was part of his plan to be rid of her forever, and it calmed me. At the least, it'd be free entertainment. We all knew he had to appease her, or she'd ruin the entire night.

I stayed on the stump, frowning a bit pensively, and Dorey returned with her date and an extra beer for me. I wasn't one to drink, but heck—I wasn't going to turn this one down. Anything to ease my nerves at this point was welcomed!

"Kate, don't worry about her. You know he's going to make sure he puts her in her place once and for all. He'll say he forgives her, she'll feel like she's won, and you'll never have to deal with her again," Dorey told me.

"Dor, I don't know. I never trusted her. I still don't, and I never will," I worriedly confided in my friend. Her date was silent and internally agreed with me. I could read it on his face.

Dorey continued, "Look, they're right there. She's probably telling him some nonsense this very second, and he's just listening—not buying it—but being kind because that's who he is. Don't you buy it either.

She's not worth your time." Dorey tried convincing us but I think at this point she was trying to convince herself as well.

When Dorey had finished a few more reassuring comments, a few of our other farm pals had taken up seats around us. Perhaps they saw our hesitation and wanted to be protective of their own kind. It did help comfort me. Not to mention, the beer probably relaxed me a bit. Maybe a bit too much because I got so lost in the conversation, that a half hour passed, and I realized Will was still gone. Still laughing at a good joke by one of the guys, I looked over where'd I'd last seen him standing with Kitty, but my laughed stopped when I realized they were missing. I excused myself to go find him, but Dorey got up and reminded me, "Don't let her get under your skin. It's what she wants. Don't end all this time, years and years of school, by letting her get the final say. He's probably just peeing in the woods!" Dorey had a way of making me laugh. She was right. And Will was a man. He knew how to handle himself. What did I have to worry about?

Another twenty minutes passed, and even Dorey couldn't keep me from wandering off at that point. She did try, but I was too concerned. I walked back to the spot they'd been at, and a few school pals looked at me with strange looks on their faces. From behind me, coming out of the woods, I could hear Kitty laughing this horrid, sweet-yet-wily giggle. From behind her own voice, came Will's. My heart sank. *What was he still doing with her, and why did he seem happy?* For a moment, I thought I was drunk. *It was just the beer speaking*, I tried to talk myself through the disgust and pit in my stomach. But I couldn't lie to myself. I'd barely had a full can!

Their voices got louder as they came out of the woods, but Will's seemed alien. It wasn't a voice I'd heard him talk in ever before. Unlike me, he *did* sound drunk, but he'd only had the same amount to drink as me. (Or at least I thought.) When they wandered out of the woods, Kitty looked messy, guilty almost. She stared right in my face as she shoved her way by me to go for the cooler. The beer Will had walked off with was gone and had been replaced with a red plastic cup she'd given him. He stumbled a bit, and some punch looking drink spilled out. He put his hand on the tailgate of a truck where I'd ended up and looked at me with a strange daze of confusion, but unable to talk. His look continued to Kitty, and he still looked dazed. I looked at her too, and then she smiled at him saying, "Glad we had a chance to make amends." She winked at me, and then walked away. *What had she done to him!*

It took everything in my body not to punch her in the face, but at that point Dorey had found me once again and looked even more confused—and frightened—by the look on my face. As Dorey tried to read me, and I tried to read Will, he seemed to try and focus on something, anything. He didn't look like himself. He didn't act like himself. As I looked him over to make sure she hadn't stabbed him or something, I noticed something on his sweatshirt collar: a spot of lipstick. The pink lipstick Kitty had always worn, which made her look rather plastic-like, was on Will. *This wasn't happening.* My head started spinning. Dorey noticed too and her mouth dropped open.

I stumbled back, feeling like I'd get sick, and had to catch myself on the tailgate as well. Most people were confused: maybe by the scene, or maybe by their intoxication. For me, I wanted to throw up. I tried to look him in the eyes, but he wouldn't look at me. He looked sick himself, and I felt numb. It took strength to stand upright, and I fumbled for a second for my keys, and when I found them, I bolted for the truck in the fastest walk I could muster since my legs were too stiff to run. Dorey tried to stop me, but I kept charging away like a bull. She was forced to help upright Will anyway, as he'd started to fall like paint dripping down a wall. Her date came to help too, as did a few other friends, and she turned to see me too far away to catch up. She knew I wasn't drunk, but she knew I was not in a mental state clear enough to drive either. A few concerned friends reached out in concern as I darted by back to where we'd parked our vehicles in an open area of the woods, but I walked by them forcefully. I ripped open the truck door, about knocking myself out. I jumped in, sat for a second to breathe in and out deeply and quickly, with a raging confusion racing through my head. The breathing that Will had taught me to clear my head wasn't working. I started the truck: turned around with sand going everywhere and started to head back the few miles to the main road. I regained my composure halfway back, at least enough to look out for wildlife that I might hurt with reckless driving. But it was me who was hurt. I was hurting so bad.

Once I had slowed, and having almost made it to the main road, I rolled a window down. It was complete black of night again. Silence was all around, and I needed fresh air to breath. I felt like I was choking. Things even seemed blurry, so I stopped the truck completely before pulling out on the main road. I just sat for a minute to get the strength to drive away. At least I had the common and ingrained sense to look both ways before pulling out on the highway to nowhere. Not like anyone even drove out in these parts, especially at this time of night. I pulled out after checking both ways. When I saw two lights coming at me quickly, I figured they were a side effect of all the horrid images racing through my mind. The lights got brighter in a matter of seconds though, and after a loud horn seemed to scream in my ear, everything went black.

Chapter 13:

BETWEEN ASLEEP AND AWAKE

The sound of the other truck hitting my own was enough to be heard for miles. Those back at the bonfire, no matter how intoxicated, were immediately sobered, and jumped up from their respective seats in a jolt. Even Will, in whatever state he was in, seemed to have snapped out of it. Dorey had been helping him walk and find his words, but the second that crash echoed through the forest, he ripped his arm from hers, and stood up straight. He still couldn't speak clearly, and started to try and run, but he couldn't. He turned to Dorey, with the most pleading eyes she'd ever seen. She knew what he meant. He was begging for help, and she couldn't turn him down. They both knew something terrible had happened, and he needed to find out what. In his gut, he knew I was in trouble. She was his only way of getting to me.

She hurriedly helped him into her SUV and drove as fast as she could down the road to find the scene. The other truck had abandoned the crash and left me in what was left of my own. When they arrived, Will jumped out of the SUV before Dorey even had time to stop, and he ran to my truck to find me. The driver's side door was crumbled shut, so he ran, feet slipping out where the sand met the asphalt, to get to the door around the other side. Dorey called 911 for help. When he opened the door frantically, he saw my body first, and then my closed eyes. I was lying lengthwise in a pool of my own blood on the bench seat. He turned around facing away from the truck, heaving up whatever poison had been in his body. Seeing me like that immediately made him sick. He wiped his mouth with the back of his sleeve, turned back around, and cried touching my wet hair.

"Oh my God! Oh my God! Someone please help!" he screamed, looking around frantically. He was helpless: to himself, to me, to anyone. "Dorey! No, no, no!" He was grasping his head with both hands, clinging to his hair like life support.

Dorey stood by his side, also seemingly powerless, but she knew help was on the way, and let him know this. She told Will to take off his sweatshirt and hold it on my head to stop the bleeding. He did it without hesitation, remaining only in a white undershirt, yet still in shock. They both noticed that my leg was shaped in an unnatural position and must have been badly broken. Dorey told him to put pressure on my head and not to move. He was beginning to come out of his comatose state quickly since having thrown up. Dorey went to look through the window of the driver's side to make sure my leg bones hadn't punctured my skin. That would mean more blood loss. Luckily, they hadn't. More people had shown up running from the bonfire, and a few had piled into the back of a truck, too. No matter who had been drinking, they had all become clearheaded very quickly. They watched Will, a normally composed guy, cry downwardly trying to focus on me, while still trying to steady my head and keep the pressure on my gash. No one could speak at the sight of it all as they all pulled up one by one.

The sirens began quietly, and then lights could be seen too as they got louder. When the help arrived, they took over. It all seemed like a nightmare for Will as he stood back watching them try to move me, diagnose the situation, stop the bleeding. When I was lifted from my truck to a stretcher, and then to the ambulance, Will jumped into it without thought. They didn't hesitate to let him stay, as he looked unwavering, and willing to put up any fight to stay by my side. The doors of the ambulance closed to a crowd of silent and horrified faces and drove off into a black night.

The nearest hospital seemed like days away as the ride went on. Will was still lost for the entirety of it: in a nightmare seeing me lay on a soft white table, and his own sickened state that was so confusing to him and keeping him from wanting to help to his fullest. What he didn't know was that he'd already kept me from bleeding to death, and there was nothing more he could do. It wasn't his fault.

There wasn't more anyone could do until we pulled into the emergency room, so when another EMT saw that Will was covered in blood he reached out to examine him as well. Something was wrong with Will for sure, but the blood on Will's shirt wasn't his, and Will told them he'd not been in the truck anyway. They realized he was covered in my blood from trying to help. He told them he'd only had half a beer, but at that point wasn't sure himself. The medics assumed he was just recovering from too much alcohol; one gave him a bottle of water and then returned to my side to help stabilize me for the rest of the ride.

Back at the campsite, the fire was extinguished, and the joy of the night had disappeared. Everyone silently packed up, or just sat around watching the fire die. Dorey watched Kitty out of the corner of her eye, with an even more scathing look than Kitty herself could have conjured. Kitty nervously packed up, trying to appear helpful and worried about me, but Dorey knew something wasn't right. Dorey walked over to stand next to a large tree, managing to keep out of Kitty's sight, and watched as Kitty dumped a bottle of pills in a stream. Dorey couldn't believe it. *Kitty was taking drugs?* As sirens approached, Dorey knew then that Kitty was rushing to clean up her illegal garbage to avoid getting caught. *How selfish!* Instead of worrying about a classmate en route to the emergency room, she was covering her own tail. Dorey was horrified but had to walk away from Kitty when the cops showed up. She'd witnessed more than anyone with the accident and needed to tell them all she knew.

Once at the hospital, the stifling chaos continued. I'd still not woken up, but I had a pulse. I was taken down a hallway, and Will was directed to the waiting room. He sat with his one leg bopping up and down rapidly, with his cowboy boot heal clinking the floor each time. He'd still not opened the water bottle the medic had given him but gripped it in his hand like something to hold on to and keep him stable. His white t-shirt had blood all over it, as did his forearms. He was still blurry and confused, but the part that was clearer to him now was just how badly injured I really was. I was lucky to be alive, and he knew it. He also blamed himself. Had he never wandered off [which he still didn't know where he'd even gone and for how long], I wouldn't have been at the hospital at all, seemingly lifeless and completely still. He kept telling himself these things over and over in his head. The one picture that kept popping up in his mind was how beautiful I looked. If even covered in blood, broken, and bent, I was beautiful to him.

Narby showed up as fast as she could, with Will's dad driving. The second Will made eye contact with her, he broke down again: collapsing into her arms, whimpering "sorry" over and over. She'd spoken with a police officer on the phone as she headed over, and the officer had told her Will was not involved in any way: not hurt, nor at any fault, as Dorey had confirmed. On both accounts, she was relieved and tried to share that little bit of comfort with Will by holding him and stroking his head as if he were ten years old again. Will's dad had tears in his eyes and stayed off to the side to hide them. He was never much to show emotion, but it was hard to hide now. I was like his family too, and this had hit him hard.

It seemed like hours passed before a doctor came out to talk to them. When she did, Will was the first to jump to his feet. He didn't have questions, but his pleading eyes spoke volumes: begging the doctor to fill them in as thoroughly and quickly as possible.

Her words seemed in slow-motion, even though each was crystal clear: "She will live, but we had to induce a coma. She is so badly injured, and we are afraid of furthering possible brain trauma, so we hadn't any other choice. We don't know the outcome but are glad you are here for her. No one can see her yet. We must keep her completely stable until you can. There is nothing we can do now but wait."

Wait. The words were like being tied to a cold metal chair for Will. No one said anything but just nodded in thanks and utter shock at the doctor. *Was this really happening?* thought Will. He was still in disbelief that any of this had even transpired in the first place. The last thing he could remember clearly was standing up next to me before he walked off with Kitty, and how I smiled up at him with worry. He had winked back assuring me everything would be okay. But he never came back, and now I was close to death. The thought that he was the one who caused me to end up practically lifeless made him sick to his stomach.

Will, Narby, and his dad stayed for at least twelve hours, and came up with a plan to take shifts after that. They still needed to eat and sleep to be at their strongest when I woke up. But Will refused. He wouldn't leave the hospital; he wouldn't eat. The nurses had told him to drink water, or he'd be forced to have an IV for fluid. His father brought him clean clothes, and a nurse was able to find him an empty hospital room in which to finally shower. As he did, he stared at the blood rinsing down the drain. He was horrified and couldn't blink. Days started passing, and he was consumed by exhaustion and hunger. But the worry of my slipping away forever kept him from dozing off completely, even when he would succumb to the tiredness. If he tried to eat, he would become nauseous. Drinking to flush out whatever he'd ingested when hanging out with Kitty, was all that kept him from dehydration.

Will started to eat after a few days but couldn't finish a full meal and was losing weight. When an entire week had passed, they were given the okay to enter my room, even though I was still in coma. Quietly, Narby came in first. But she made it as short as her heart would allow because she knew Will's pain and guilt was unbearable for him, and she knew he needed to be with me. Somehow, she knew I needed him too.

She didn't hold back tears, but she made sure to wipe them away before she left to get Will. She didn't want him thinking he'd brought pain to anyone else since he already refused to believe he wasn't the one at fault for the entire scenario in the first place.

When she exited the room, the expression on her face and nod of her head was to prepare him. She was silently telling him that it would be hard to see me like that. He understood but didn't think about that. Nothing would deter him. He wanted to touch me and feel that I was alive. He needed to know I was still breathing. For some reason, he had convinced himself that my being alive would save him, even though I was the one who was in critical condition.

When he entered, the sound of a mechanical pulse hit him hard. He didn't expect to be broken down so quickly. Beyond the sounds, came the site of me lying still. His stomach dropped. I was still attached to tubes, wires, braces, and a cast, but this time, propped up with a pillow beneath my head. I had a wrap across my forehead, and the blood had been rinsed from my hair and skin. The bruising and swelling were mostly hidden behind sheets, but one side of my face was completely black and blue. The other side, however [the one Will could see], was somehow untouched by the disaster. He focused on that, and his face didn't leave mine as he felt weakly for a chair to sit in. He looked at the soft curves on my cheek and jawline, in a faint glow coming from a little light on a table. He looked down slowly on my body, like he had my arm when I put his pin on before prom, and watched my chest rise and fall slowly, peacefully, repeatedly, and mechanically. His mouth was dry, and he realized he'd forgotten his water. He couldn't cry, he couldn't speak, and neither could he blink. There was a tingle in the back of his nose that almost felt it would push tears down his face, and his neck and arms felt weak, and numb. His legs even more so, and he was grateful for the chair—more comfortable than those in the waiting room. In the days that had passed, the poison feeling in his body had mostly washed away, but so had his color. He looked like a ghost when watching me. The nurses were constantly in and out but silently, allowing him a passive time with me and only reminding him to drink now and then. Eventually, more than one person was allowed in the room at once, and Narby would spend much time in the room with Will as well. She'd hold his hand, and remind him, "Child, this was not your fault." She tried time and time again to get him to eat a full meal. It was only after three days she'd even gotten him to eat crackers because he had almost fallen from being lightheaded.

About a week into my stillness, he finally found his words. He could finally speak, but—little did he know—I could hear it. I could hear every word. His words were weak and dry, but I heard them. We were alone in the still of the room and he knew it was time to talk to me.

"Katie." As he said my name, the tears from the night of the accident returned, and they poured down his faced. He didn't cry out loud, but the tears just kept raining down like a spring storm. He continued through his paralysis of tears, "I am holding your hand. Can you feel it? I swear to you, I wish I'd never gotten up to leave you in the woods. You are everything to me. I love you." He broke down in tears then, his head collapsing and his voice sobbing. "Please, please wake up. Let me hold you. I can't hold you when you're lying there. You're too far away. Please." His tears continued streamed down his face, never-ending. They burned his dehydrated skin, and dry lips.

For another week, it continued. He pleaded with me to come back. He held my hand. He even brought me lily-of-the-valley in a little vase. He hurt, but at least he was finally eating more, and took long naps next to me in the chair by my bed when his body would give in to the exhaustion. He took a shower each day, and Narby and his dad had brought him a bag of clothing each day too: only bringing one outfit at a time so it gave hope that the next day I'd be awake, and we'd be able to finally leave.

For me, I was somewhere trapped in the past, present, and future. I could see my childhood, our childhood. I could hear him now, and somehow, I could see things happening now too. Whether they were real or not, I could see *Dorey trying to work on her farm but struggling because of her worry for me. I could see Mr. Leeds petting Mr. Mayor on his lap in silence and deep thought. Mrs. Mill's tried to concentrate in her office but had a hard time being her normal focused self. The farmers went about their routine and just hid the thought of me never coming back to work with them. They ploughed on and spoke of it with Will's dad, like I'd be back any day helping to pick the flowers that were starting to bloom. I could smell them. I could see Narby, restless, and a nervous wreck, not the normal steadfast rock that she'd always been. Her heart broke for me, for all I'd been through in life. She couldn't believe that the worst thing that'd happened to me was out of love and me running from the thought that'd it been stolen from me.* I saw Will, thinner than he was, and gray with fatigue, his hand still holding mine, and so much that they seemed attached. I could feel him squeeze my hand, and I could feel myself squeeze back. *Or was that his hand doing all the work because I was still asleep?* I realized then that I *was* awake; I realized the flowers I smelled weren't those on the farm but rather the lilies in the vase right by my side. I realized it *was* my hand squeezing his back.

Will had just started to drift off to sleep and must have thought he imagined feeling something too. Perhaps we were both having the same dream about holding hands. I couldn't talk, and could barely turn my head, but I saw him leaning on his other hand, sitting in the chair, in front of the large window with soft light coming through. Somehow, I was able to curl the end of my mouth to smile knowing he was there. He must have sensed my eyes opening and opened his own. He sat up slowly and stared at me as if to make no sudden moves and send me back into a worsened state than I already was.

He whispered, "Katie. I'm here. You're going to be okay. You're okay." He tried holding back tears to stay strong, and sheer relief was all that gave him that strength.

He'd begged me repeatedly when I was in the coma not to leave him. He'd asked if I was here. But now to hear him tell me I was alive, I was with him, and that I'd be okay, solidified that I was and would be. The other corner of my mouth curled, but they both collapsed again, and my eyes cringed when I felt the effects of the accident hit me all at once. When a nurse came in for the routine check, her eyes widened, and she smiled and nodded. She rushed back out to get the doctor. A few came back in with the nurse. Will stood out of the way now, smiling with tears in his eyes and holding his chest as they checked over me. It took a while, but he sat still and watched patiently as they examined. A weight like never before had been lifted from him.

After my health assessment, another stipulation was put on our visits, as to little physical contact other than a held hand or gentle caress of my hair so I could be monitored. But Will spoke to me and let me talk and hold his hand when I had the strength again. He told me everything that had happened. I made him promise to eat, and he gave me privacy when Narby came to help me change and start to sit up fully again. I would need therapy, of course, and it was a miracle I could even move. The stitch-covered cuts on my leg were healing nicely, even so soon after the accident, but it would be weeks before I could even put any weight on the healing bones. But this was all direction and news from the staff. Will was more focused on when he could touch me closer again, give me a hug, or hold me.

Another week passed, and it was nearing a time Will could finally get his wish. As I slept one night, he watched my hand. He didn't touch it though. He looked at my body breathing on its own, with no more wires or tubes. He watched the monitor that was now quieter in volume and watched my healing face. Except for stitches, and the faint bruising still on one side, I looked like myself again. He kept watching me, and then quietly scooted his chair closer. He stood as if to leave, but then crouched down next to the bed, and bent over. He couldn't stay away any longer. Next to my forehead stitches, and then next to each bruise he could see on my arms, he kissed me gently. Then back to my face and head, he kissed me everywhere but my mouth. Perhaps he knew I was susceptible to illness since I was so weak, or maybe he didn't want to feel like he was taking advantage of me while I slept. The fact is, when that moment would come that he would kiss me, he wanted it to be ours, not just his. But one thing he couldn't hold back, and when he spoke the words softly, manly, and directly, I heard it close to my ear and it was very clear it wasn't a dream: "I love you, Katie. I've loved you from the moment I met you, and I'm going to love you forever."

Chapter 14:
A LOCK WITH NO KEY

That summer, recovery was like a visit to the past. Will slowly helped me regain my strength with many patient trips helping me walk through the woods, swims at the waterhole, and—my favorite—a hammock he'd installed beneath the willow at Narby's. We spent hours and hours lying side by side, talking about our past, our present, and the future. Before we'd gotten to the latter, he'd made sure to tell me more details of what had happened that night: especially with Kitty and their wandering off together.

Under a warm summer breeze, so appropriate and soothing for the time of year, he told me one evening, "Dorey reached out to me." His eyes looked shamed.

I was concerned for him, for her, for me, and for what he was about to say. I looked at him longingly with that same concern and let him go on.

He continued, "Kitty had drugged me. That night in the woods, before the accident, she slipped pills in my drink and drugged me." His face was a mixture of hurt, guilt, embarrassment, and complete fury. The combination of feelings had been eating him alive since Dorey made him aware of this news. It was shocking to me too, and brought on the same emotions that he felt, but all he'd done to bring me back to good health and happiness once again, I knew right at that moment to ask him if he was okay, and just move on. But he had some more to say first.

"All this time, I let her walk all over me, over us. Just to save my dad's job. I love my dad. But I love you too. You are both my family. Dorey asked me what I wanted to tell Kitty, and I said I'd tell her myself. But Dorey was steadfast about keeping me away from her, and willingly put herself in the middle to keep her away from us. She is in the process—maybe even at this very moment—of meeting Kitty at her barn, to tell her never to contact us again because if she does, I will press charges against Kitty for what she did. That should be enough to keep her away and save my dad's job, too. I still don't even know what happened when I was alone with her, but I believe it was all a set-up and nothing happened. We never have to see her again, Katie. It's over."

When he was finished, an air between us had been cleared. Although all these years we'd never let her come between us, there was always the underlying threat of when she'd strike next. But it was over. She had struck for the last time.

As we laid there continuing to go over details of my accident (that I was finally prepared to hear), an unexpected sight rolled up. On the back of a flatbed truck was my own. Crumbled on one side like a piece of paper to be tossed in the trash. We were both confused as to why it was there. Narby got out of the passenger side of the flatbed and gave direction for the driver to follow her to the boathouse. There, she slid open the doors, and gave him further direction to unload the mess of a vehicle down from the bed, and into a [possibly final] resting place. The man nodded and waited for more of his crew to arrive so they could help. She saw us on the hammock, gave a sad smile, and then walked back to the porch and into the house. We understood. It was a look to say, "I can't believe all you've been through Kate, and how in the world you survived this." I knew the truck was only there because she probably had intent to restore it one day. But to see it like that made me shiver.

Will couldn't bite his tongue, and had to say it out loud, maybe even to believe himself, "You're alive. I don't know how you are alive."

He reached over to squeeze my hand, and I looked over at him to give him a slight smile to let him know I was okay and not going anywhere. He dropped a leg from the hammock and gave the ground a push to put us back into a lazy rocking, and we laid side by side in silence, taking it all in and knowing it was time to move on. I'd been through too much in life, and we just wanted to move on… together.

A while later, Narby emerged from the house with some chicken wings she'd made. They were one of the favorite treats she made us, but me having been in no shape to handle any food other than mild and bland kept us from the fiery delights. But no longer did we have to avoid them. It was perfect timing, too. We were hungry. Once he helped me walk to the picnic table, Will dug in first. Normally, he'd have waited for the ladies to start, but he was a hungry man who had gone too long without real food. Watching him devour the chicken was hilarious. He was covered in sauce immediately: hands and mouth. I watched him for a while before he realized it, and I just cracked up in laughter. He frowned with his eyes, but then smiled all the same with a mouth that resembled a clown, just to humor me so he could get back to chowing down. Plates later of more eating, he was good and full. He had gone through about a dozen paper towels to clean himself and a few dozen wings as well, and sat back in satisfaction.

I had to chime in. "Will, I don't think I've ever seen you this hungry."

"Katie, my dear, a man needs meat. I haven't gotten some good bones to gnaw on for a month," he growled and put his hands up with fingers bent as if to show bear paws.

I adored him. His effort to humor me, his lightheartedness how he could laugh at himself, and still never worrying about what others thought about him. He knew I wasn't one who would ever think anything less than pure love for him, so he never held back: not emotion, not mannerisms, not a single thought. He was one in a million. How something so simple as watching him eat spicy chicken wings was warming, made me smile, and tilt my head in thought. This boy lived for me. I never wanted it to end, so I thought it was a good time to let him know, it wasn't going to. In fact, I felt like letting him know just how serious I was about staying by his side and showing him I lived for him too.

"I think you should know something," I said. He looked a little concerned but listened intently all the same while he licked the last bits of buffalo sauce off his fingertips.

"I heard back from all the colleges I applied to. As you know, I applied to one in New England, and the rest around here." I made my face serious in a way to show I might bring some bad news. I was just being playful of course and letting him worry for a second to screw around like old times, but I couldn't let him wonder too long. "Anyway, I'll be a half hour away, and commuting." He knew then I'd chosen the closest school. It was a good school and had been hard to get into. It would mean a lot of work and studying, but most of all—it meant we'd never be apart.

He flung the dirty paper towels into the air, "Woohoo! Congratulations!" I think his words were more out of congrats for himself knowing he was important enough to get his girl to stay close, but he was truly happy for me as well. He came over to pick me up and give me a hug but reminded himself to be gentle since I wasn't one hundred percent back to myself yet.

The day had ended perfectly. We were back to us: a place of calm, peace, and having each other in our own little world. It was a humble world, but ours all the same.

The next morning came around like all those of the summer had. I prepared for my physical therapy in the form of walks and water led by Will. Perhaps at this point I was milking it a bit, and just enjoying being picked up, and piggy backing with Will. His touch was so gentle and caring, and it just felt so good to be loved. He was always there for me.

Always had been. He never missed a second to show up, as if he were in tune to my anticipating when he would. And at that very minute, he arrived. The doorbell rang, and I hobbled as fast as I could to open the door.

Expecting to find him standing with those gleaming blue eyes, I was taken aback to find them glazed over and staring at my feet; set in a morose face, seemingly void of expression. His skin was pale, like how he looked when I'd first opened my eyes in the hospital. I stood there for [at least what felt like] an eternity, frozen with apprehension.

"Will? What's wrong?" I placed my hands on his shoulders to steady him.

He finally found the strength to meet my eyes with his own and spoke slowly, seeming to almost need to hear them out loud to believe himself. "It's my dad."

"Oh god, Will. What happened?" I asked, assuming the worst.

He continued looking in my eyes, and they seemed to sink even further into his soul. "He was fired." His eyes dropped again.

In part relief that it wasn't something to do with his father's health, but part pity that he was now jobless I tried to get him to look back at me so I could console him. But I could feel him tense, and as he lifted his eyes back to connect with mine, I could tell something more was coming. It seemed he had been crying, and any color that was left in his face disappeared when he said it, "Kitty. She's pregnant." His voiced cracked then, "She said it's mine."

The moment between us following his statement was like a death sentence. There were no words, there was no emotion; only numbness. We became almost strangers. Or perhaps lost souls who knew they couldn't help each other anymore. *He had slept with Kitty that night. That was the part he couldn't remember.*

Having forgotten my hands were still on his shoulders, I dropped them. I didn't move them. They just lost their muscle tone and dropped. I became a zombie then. My parents dying: an accident. But this was intent. What she had done to him—to us—was intentional. And he was the other half of that intent. He had hurt me intentionally. The invisible wall I built between us was immediate and made of steel. I was left staring into a metal reflection of hurt in my own eyes. I turned, robotically back into the house. He was left standing alone in the doorway and had no words. He felt the wall too, and all he could do was stare for a moment as I walked off. He backed up, slowly and dizzily, almost falling backward down the porch stairs. The screened porch door shut softly with a creak from the hinge after I'd turned to walk away, and I shut the inner door, locking it. Then and there, I locked Will out of my life.

He had intended on walking home but ended up wandering aimlessly in the woods. Things raced through his mind, but he couldn't cry or get angry. Strength was drained from him. I hurt, but he hurt too. Perhaps I should have been more sympathetic, but he didn't try to stay and apologize, or explain. He didn't try to reach out and hold me. He had no more words. He just left. He wanted to strangle Kitty, thank Dorey, and apologize to her for having gotten stuck in the middle of all this mess, and run back to my farm to break down the door and drop to his knees to beg me for forgiveness. But he couldn't do a thing. He was paralyzed and could only wander like a lost little boy. He'd let me down, his father down, and himself down. He'd always felt like being a good person and treating others with kindness meant life was good. But he'd hurt the one person he loved most, and he felt that all good had been stolen from him. I didn't know how he felt of course, and only assumed he didn't care that he'd just emotionally knocked the wind out of me. For a moment, I thought maybe I was still in the coma, in a nightmare. But it was real, and somehow I felt more like death than when I was actually near dying.

I found my way up the old wooden stairs to my room and methodically started packing. I didn't know where I was going, but I had to get out of there, out of that town.

Narby entered the house a bit startled after a run to the grocery store, having found the front door locked. We never locked the door, and it had worried her. She put a carton of milk down on a little table in the foyer and hurried up the steps.

"Kate, what's going on?" She got to the doorway of my room. "And why are you packing?" She stood with her arms drooping in front of her, coming together with loosely folded hands at the bottoms. She was trying to figure out how to help, leaning in like Mrs. Mills always had and trying to be a good listener. I refused to talk and kept packing. Figuring I was at least alive, and the house hadn't been burglarized, she assumed whatever my issue was one that could surely be talked through. But she had no idea that this "issue" was not just an issue. It was the end to what had become the biggest part of my life. And when I finally opened to talk, she was left with parted lips and little words. Only asking again, but more softly this time and already knowing the answer, "Why are you packing?"

I came up with my answer on the spot, and replied immediately, "I changed my mind. I'm going to New England for school." I was defiant, and dead serious. She knew it, too. Once a stubborn child, always a stubborn child. When I made up my mind, I stuck with the plan. Whether even truly thinking through the consequences, the immediate escape was more important. I'd deal with anything else later. But at that moment, I had to get out of there. My plan didn't just affect me though. It affected Narby, too. Though she'd not outwardly said so, my staying around for college would have been comforting for her, not just Will. In fact, I knew just how much this affected her when she tried to be strong and said with a little hesitation and a shaky and apprehensive voice, "I'll help you find a place. I have an old friend who retired up there years ago. We'd sailed the Caribbean together in college when we were just a bit older than you, and I bet she'll know someone looking to rent out an apartment."

I nodded my head to silently answer *yes*. Narby was satisfied enough, but as she looked at the pile of things I was packing, she noticed I'd left something aside on my nightstand.

She asked, "Kate, what about your journal?"

For so long, I'd written of my adventures with Will. Page after page was filled with every memory we'd made together. She'd not known what I wrote about, only that I spent much time writing in it. Had she known, I'm sure she'd have not asked.

I turned to face her, and spoke sternly, "Burn it."

By the week's end, we'd loaded up a new truck Narby had purchased shortly after the wreck, and we headed north. I was leaving my home behind and my childhood in the rear-view mirror.

Chapter 15:
TOWN BY THE SEA

I arrived in coastal New England on a late afternoon in mid-August before my freshman year. Luckily for me, I'd somehow still managed to get in on my initial acceptance letter. It had been too late to join the sailing team, but that was the last thing on my mind anyway. All I could think of was the escape. Sight unseen, I had based my future home of education on photos, and its reputation for a good journalism program. In person, the place far-exceeded the photographs, and I was star-struck by the harbor town immediately. The nautical history was built with red brick and cobblestone sidewalks, wharf shops with a familiar cedar shake siding, smells of fresh seafood being grilled in restaurants deep-rooted in the community, and people walking around with cable knit sweaters around their shoulders—prepared for the fresh chilly air that would blow in with the fog come sundown. The air was mixed with salt and an occasional and familiar hint of fuel from the yachts filling up along the docks. Fancy antique convertibles were snuggled in here and there along the street edges. These, of course, caught Narby's eye. She had this funny taste for all things antique and shiny. Hours passed with both of us mesmerized by this place I was about to call home for the next four years. As we wandered, I just tried to keep my mind off all I'd left behind.

That evening, we met up with Narby's friend. As she had mentioned, they'd met in their twenties and had been old sailing buddies.

Their reunion was grand: laughs, hugs, yelling out with old jokes, all without a care who witnessed the affair. They were like sisters. They didn't leave me a third wheel though. I was sister number three as soon as the old friend laid eyes on me, and then and there I was welcomed as family just the same. Thank goodness she'd found a place for me after all.

Well into the night, we were given the grand tour. Restaurants, houses, sight-seeing, and boats. All the nautical splendors were in front of my eyes; sailing yachts I'd only ever dreamt of or saw in pictures were within fingers reach. The best part: college was built on the edge of town, so this new stomping ground would be mine. My daily morning view would be all I'd just toured. Just like I did when I'd first moved to the Pine Barrens, I would have the time to adventure and experience everything new. But this time, I would do it alone, and I wasn't going to wallow in self-pity. I would be a grown woman, in need of no help. I didn't *need* anyone. For a moment that thought saddened me, but I shook it off as quickly as I could.

Narby stayed in town for the rest of the weekend and headed out the same day as her friend once they'd gotten me set up in an apartment near the wharf. They'd been nice enough to find a place for me last minute, and even better—rent free. Another old pal had taken me in, and it was just an added show of kindness from one sailor to another, I'd supposed. I was to stay there a few weeks before school started, until my dorm would be open for me to move in. Maybe I was silly to have left only two weeks before school started, but I just couldn't stay. Narby never questioned it, and she understood more than anyone. She had seen me grow up alongside of that person I called my other half. And she saw something in me die at the end of that relationship. It was reason enough to move out and move on; or at least try to.

The weeks of wandering in my new town were prosperous. I returned with welcome to the places we'd gone to eat when Narby and her friend had first shown me around town and found some new places on my own as well. Since I had no connection to the place and no family there either, familiar places and friendly faces made living there feel comforting and welcoming. It made me feel part of the town, and I reveled knowing I felt safely harbored, without even having anchored down quite yet. The best part: I was doing it all on my own.

School came fast, and it was easy for me to gather the few things I'd had at the wharf apartment to relocate to my dorm. In fact, a golf cart lent to me by a local acquaintance was all I needed to load up my belongings and head just down the street and up the hill to my next residence. It helped that it had a row-boat on wheels attached to the back for extra space! New England was turning out to be fun, and it was only the beginning. I hadn't even met my roommate yet.

I'd only known her name from a letter in the mail, but nothing else. I wondered how I'd find her, but I didn't have to: she found me first.

About four inches taller than me, stood a busty and beautiful red head outside the dorm. As I pulled up, she smiled eagerly, "Kate?"

I chuckled at the way she said it, with hands on her hips, and this little twist and grin, so sparkling and fashionable. From head to toe, she was the total opposite of me: designer clothing, a purse to match, perfectly done hair and make-up, and a nail polish color just as bright and glittery as her personality. This girl had money, but unlike girls such as Kitty and the yachtie kids from the island, she had love too. I could sense it. She had a heart and gave everyone a fair chance, no matter where they came from or what their monetary value was. This was obvious since I was wearing simple jean shorts, a tee shirt, and my hair up in a messy ponytail, as she still pulled me in for a hug. At least I wasn't covered in dirt like my childhood days! Those days were over now, and this was my new life.

"Girlfriend get your cute little butt over here, and give your new sister a squeeze," she said.

She released me from her perfumed snuggle, and stepped back, still holding my forearms, and taking in her new friend with smiling approval. I might not have been cut from the same cloth, but I would do just fine.

"Skipper! I've been looking forward to meeting you, too," I said and I held her arms in my own. "Wish we'd gotten a chance to know each other before move in day," I added, laughing a little.

"Oh sweetie, this just gives us a reason to go out for lunch and shopping to officially bond!" She was pleased with her words but needed to live up to them. "First, we need to get your stuff inside." She waved to a man in a suit, who speedily walked our way. *Oh, good lord, who was I rooming with?*

Somehow this man reminded me of Mayor the skunk: you didn't quite know what was going through his mind, but his loyalties were clearly to the person in charge of him, all whilst dressed in a black and white suit!

"Miss Skipper?" he spoke at her service.

A short introduction left me wondering if there was more to come. But that was it. He was the man with no name and a nice black and white suit. That was it.

"Nice to meet you," I said looking at him.

He nodded, asking me where I'd like my bags. I wasn't sure what to do, and actually—felt a little awkward. I had the health and strength to move my own things, so this was all new to me. However, I probably didn't have my complete strength back just yet, so I welcomed the help. Skipper answered for me, "Same room, dear," and then she perked up proudly with her arm around my shoulder, "My new roomie! Isn't she cute?" Her teeth were almost unnaturally white behind some very plump lips. Many things were plump on her in fact, and I wondered if they were real or not.

"Yes, Miss," he confirmed to Skipper. Off he went like one of the chipmunks from back home: scurrying in a fashion as if to prepare for winter and gathering as much as he could in one round to store away in the unknown. I hadn't even seen my room yet, and was being pulled by a pretty, life-sized doll down the street by my forearm.

She was delighted to be my tour guide.

"Okay, so you're going to love this restaurant. When my parents come to town, this is our favorite spot." She continued, perhaps feeling like she needed to explain the absence of her family. "They're at a golf charity this weekend, so they sent our butler." (*That explained Mr. No Name!*) "My parents both met at school here, so I know the town and people here well." She seemed proud and let down all at the same time. Maybe this is what the preppy kids from sailing school felt: abandonment by their parents because they had other engagements that were more important that their own kids.

She continued again, "What about your mother and father?"

"Well, they've both passed. Narby, who had dropped me off, is sort of my combined mom and dad." I chuckled, being able to smile at the memory of my parents and share my gratitude for Narby out loud with my new friend. "I hope you can meet her soon."

"How sweet!" she proclaimed. Everything with Skipper was flashing eyes, dainty, and frilled fingers flamboyantly waving in the air, and movements only a model on a runway could pull off. Everywhere we went, people just stared. I assumed it was at her, but she chimed in at some point, "Well, isn't the new girl quite the eye-catcher."

"Who? Me?" I was caught off guard and completely oblivious. She smiled and winked at me. Obviously, she was completely proud that she'd found me before everyone else. Maybe they looked at me because – like always – I didn't fit into the crowd. But she insisted, "You are just adorable. What an all-American cutie you are! Where do you get your lashes done?"

Say, what now?

"Uhh…," I managed to drawl out. But before I could finish, she bustled me into the door past a long line of waiting patrons, and right to the hostess desk to the aforementioned watering hole. Oh brother, I felt so bad. I was so accustomed to being modest, and I didn't want my few weeks of building fast, friendly acquaintances around town based on kind character, to now being overshadowed by the company I kept and being seemingly more important that everyone else by cutting in lines.

"Right this way," said an older woman who was most likely local, and seated us out on the deck over-looking the harbor when she recognized Skipper. It was an entirely different view from this point. I thought I'd seen everything there was to see in my prior weeks of wandering, but apparently the elite had hidden vantage points locked away from the rest of us.

"Oh wow! What a pretty view!" I said and was in awe looking down over dozens of white sailboats and yachts moored in the bright blue water.

When a waitress finally came over, Skipper was fast to put in our drink order, "Two Shirley temples, please," she said and smiled with perfect dimples.

"I don't think I've had one of those since I was a kid," I giggled.

She grinned shyly now, squinting her big brown eyes, "Babe, they are not for kids, trust me."

As the waitress put down our drinks a few minutes later, and Skipper sent her back on her way again after politely asking for a little more time to look over the menu, she fumbled around in her big designer bag, "Ah! Here we go." Out she pulled a little bottle of vodka. "Makeshift martinis, my dear!" she noted.

My eyes widened and I laughed internally as she took away the virginity of her drink and she cocked her head, winking.

I smiled. How could I not? Then, my eyes widened as she poured the rest of the vodka in my own drink. She followed, "Cheers, babe!"

Oh, what the heck, I thought. It'd been one heck of a summer; I deserved a drink. I was in a fancy harbor town, so maybe it was time to give up the backwoods beer and indulge in a little seaside libation.

"Cheers!" I smiled.

Two hours later, after fresh oysters, a charcuterie board, and a few more cocktails, we had given each other life stories, and became fast friends. Drinking something stronger than a simple beer had me blabbering like a fool, and goodness only knows what all I said! I only hoped I didn't say anything about a certain young man I was trying hard to forget. I was pretty sure I hadn't. But to help me forget about him, I focused on a gorgeous and lustrous sailing yacht pulling up to the dock instead.

A group of guys about our age [I presumed], roped up below the restaurant deck in the harbor. They caused quite the stir just like the yuppies from my island days and seemed to catch the attention of any female within their sound range. They were cute. No doubt. Skipper was delighted to have the company of some attractive yachties pull up, but she fully pretended not to care. Her nonchalance was bogus perhaps, but mine was genuine. I was just happy to be surrounded by a nice nautical town in the presence of a new friend, and didn't care the slightest bit about the new male additions to the harbor. In fact, I was hoping they wouldn't see me as my attire was [once again in life] the opposite of the crowd. How funny when I had gone to a low-key town, I'd dressed up fancy for my first day of class, and now—here I was at a fancy restaurant in jeans and a t-shirt! The boat was sure keeping my attention though, and my attire was the last thing on my mind. *What a good-looking boat!* I thought.

The sailors docked: securing all ropes and hopping off to come to the same restaurant we were at to grab their own lunch. Somehow, after a day of sailing, their hair was perfect, and their shirts without a wrinkle. I couldn't figure out why these guys were dressed like this. Sailing was a relaxing hobby or sport, not a luxury, at least to me. I always went in bare feet, a bathing suit, and a simple cover up, not fancy pants and pressed shirts.

No sooner having come up the dock stairs and seeing us enjoying our drinks and last bits of lunch, did one of the handsome crew members headed our way. He boldly pulled up a chair next to Skipper and the mutual flirting was instantaneous. So much for her front!

Seeing they were welcome, the rest of the guys made their way over as well. New friends, all around. And… they sailed. Any sailor was a friend of mine, and clearly no one cared what I was wearing. Phew!

With introductions made, the candid banter to follow was spiked on their end as well, as they'd already been drinking on their respective boat.

One of the guys with bright blond, manicured hair was a little more liberated by libation than the others, and just yelled, "Arrr" like a pirate upon his arrival to us.

They all gave some hearty laughs at his cheesy commentary, and a toast to solidify their brotherhood. It was completely corny, and they knew it. I discretely rolled my eyes.

As they continued their rants, trying to impress us with their wondrous seafaring skills, their boat itself started to drift away from the dock. No one seemed to notice, but I sure did.

It must have been the liquor talking, but I boldly spoke up.

I looked directly at the lead guy's eyes, tilted my head toward their yacht, keeping my eyes on his, "Your pirate skills seemed to have overlooked those of your knot-tying. Might want to try a cleat hitch next time."

He seemed to struggle a minute to take his golden-brown eyes off mine, but when he finally did, he had a chance to look over to his boat: one that was now almost six feet from the dock and unraveling very quickly from the knot he'd tied.

"No!" he sprung to his feet, knocking over Skipper's drink into her lap. Two of the guys instantly rushed to pat her dry, clearly wanting a view of her long legs, and the other two ran behind Captain Fancy Pants back down the dock to the boat. What a sight it was, watching some drunk yachties scramble to retrieve their lines. Their forty-two-foot sailing yacht was taunting them with every inch it drifted.

"Somebody's daddy is going to be angry," I laughed to myself under my breath.

The entire restaurant was now being entertained, and unison laughter broke out when Mr. Captain himself was forced to plunge in the water and drag back the ropes like a water dog. He even looked the part when he climbed back out dripping wet.

Skipper had dismissed her new friends from wiping her dry, and she leaned into my ears to whisper as she looked down on the dock, "Please let him take his shirt off." I just shook my head and laughed, rolling my eyes.

After tying the boat up a little tighter this time (and much to Skipper's delight) he peeled off his top after all, and revealed some tan, wet, washboard abs. I do believe every woman in the place was staring. Somehow my mind wandered to the time on the beach when I'd stared at Will the same way the women were all staring at this sailor. *No. No no no. I am not thinking about Will.* I tucked the memory in an internal vault in my heart, hoping never to open it again. Locked.

He walked on board the boat to change into some dry clothing, and then reemerged. The two guys who'd been with him decided to head back out into town, but captain guy came back up, tail tucked between his legs, and sat down next to me. Somehow, even after a dip in the harbor, he smelled good.

He finally started talking after we sat shoulder to shoulder, both looking ahead. He could sense me smiling with pride. "Okay, cleat hitch, any more advice?" I just kept smiling smugly.

"Hmm. Well, bathing suits usually work better for sailing, especially when you need to get wet." I wrinkled half of my nose and squinted my eyes, thoughtfully, shaking my head.

"Noted. Thank you," he said and turned to look at me, and I got a [very up close] view of those eyes now. Very handsome. Oh yes. And he knew it. But he was also fascinated with me. He was intrigued that I challenged him and didn't just fall all over him like most girls probably would have. Skipper was too busy playing mind games with her two new friends to notice our own little flirtation across the table, but there was a spark, for sure. Seemingly shocked at his manners, he stated, "My goodness, I haven't even gotten your name!"

I smiled, maybe blushing a bit like I had the first time I met Randy on the farm. "Katie," and I stuck out my hand daintily. Over the years I'd become more refined and girly. Not a girly girl like Skipper, but more feminine at least.

"I'm Brigg." Following with his last name, I knew exactly who his family was, and all they owned. Heck, they could have owned the whole darn town for all I knew! I thought he was done trying to earn back his pride from having performed such a lax job on the docking, when he continued to speak.

"So, I'll have you know, we had a few to drink when we were out sailing. I normally tie the perfect knot, so I blame the drinks. I also blame our captain and crew for seeming to have disappeared," he noted, as he looked around frowning.

"Or lack thereof the oh-so-perfect knot," I said, destroying his sense of smugness again.

"Okay, you win. I've made a scene; I get it." He had this decree of speech that made people listen and make note that he was someone prominent. His eyes rolled a bit, he seemed above and beyond his mistake, and ready to move on, all the while laughing and having a good sense of self humor. But still, he was underlyingly impressed that he wasn't winning me over; and still, he wasn't. Fact was I had no interest in dating someone like him. The rich and famous were not for me. Little did I know, I was in the center of their ring!

He spoke up again, enough to let Skipper and his pals hear him too, "Boys, the lady's lunch is on us. Least we could do for our interruption." Then, turning to me again he said, "And we'd like to invite you to a little back-to-school picnic at our house tomorrow night."

As I was about to politely decline, Skipper came and took the chair next to me, "We'd love to!" [*Darnit, Skipper!*]

Caught off-guard, and maybe a little by his pouting puppy face silently begging me to come, I concurred with my friend, "Looks like we'll see you tomorrow." I had given in. I cracked. He was satisfied. He'd gotten my attention again. The blonde fellow was very drunk at this point and couldn't help himself and chimed in with the pirate voice again, "Hey, ladies, if ya don't dangle yer bait, ya won't catch ye a mate."

I rolled my eyes with a giggle at the nautical charm to his completely nonsensical comment, and the terrible pirate impression. Skipper laughed, overly enthusiastic just to let him know she was interested. I believe the alcohol had hit all of us a little harder. *Good grief! Where did I end up at school? Would it have been this way back home? Home...*

Clearly, I was having trouble keeping my mind off what I'd run from so abruptly. Right now, they'd be harvesting the deer corn and last of the tomatoes before fall. The autumn festival would host kids running wildly through pumpkin patches in the next few weeks and corn mazes next month. *The corn... at night... with the fireflies.* I felt sick suddenly. Maybe it was the last cocktail returning to haunt me.

"Hey, are you ok?" Brigg said, and I turned to look him in the face. He looked genuinely concerned, and it was soothing.

"Oh. Yeah." I shook my head as if it were nonsense to even worry about my expression, as also to shake the thoughts from my mind. "I'm fine." I changed the subject quickly, "Anyway, looking forward to your party. *Oh great, not only was I now a drinker, but clearly a good liar, too.* I hadn't realized I'd shown my internal feelings on the outside.

Skipper and I stood to thank the guys for lunch and excuse ourselves, and—as old money gentleman—they stood up immediately to get our chairs, though it seemed more out of habit than wanting to be gracious.

I looked at handsome Brigg then. He was hard not to look at; sort of when I first saw Randy, I supposed. "Nice to have met you," I said plainly. It set him in his place again and he was back to the chase.

"Same." He shook my hand as closely as he could to my body, and I got a whiff of his pleasant scent again. I gulped, and I think he knew it. He was proud his charm was working. After an extra-long shake, he dropped my hand gently, and then walked off with his posse.

The entire way back into town, Skipper giggled with delight. "Don't you know who that was? Geez, girl, looks like you have quite the boy toy!"

Boy toy? I thought, pondering upon the notion. Clearly, she didn't know I really had no interest other than looking at him. He was candy for the eyes, but not a guy for me.

"Lucky you!" she continued enviously, but I could tell it came with not a mean bone. She was one of "them" after all, but still not with the same arrogance. If even she did show a little snobbery, it was wholly innocent. She truly was clueless. We were different, but I really liked Skipper, and I could tell she really liked me. We were fast friends, like Dorey and I were from day one.

When we strolled back into town, I learned very quickly she was easily distracted not only by cute boys, but also cute clothing.

She lit up, thrilled at her find. "Look at that!" she squealed in delight, pointing at a dress in the window of a designer clothing store.

It was the skirted version of a pair of embroidered chinos Narby had once attempted to dress me in growing up: navy with pink starfish. Somehow, I did admire the added little white country flair at the hem-line though… that somehow also resembled the curtains back home on the farm. The farm. *Oh god! This was going to be tough. Even the hem of a dress reminded me of home!*

"Come on!" she squealed, knocking any thoughts of Will from my mind. She was off to parade me around through a forest of fashion. I had gone from a world of pines to the land of luxury.

Welcome to New England, Katie.

Chapter 16:

ANOTHER SIDE OF THE BOY TOY

That night, dressed in a jumpsuit in which Skipper had found and styled me in (and insisted she pay for as a welcoming present), I felt rather spiffy; spiffy, but abnormal. I figured I'd give it a shot though. Maybe I did look "completely fab," as Skipper insisted, and it'd be perfect for the back-to-school picnic. However....

It was no picnic. It was a huge party at a frat house. No, no—a mansion. Skipper seemed in her element, I was reveling at all the beautiful architecture and history that must have been behind the place, and everyone else was just drunk.

Brigg was waiting for us on a big, raised stone patio when we arrived. His eyes and comment confirmed Skipper's choice in my style for the night. "Wow. You look... just wow!" I was flattered and smiled to show my thanks. At this point, as I'd assumed earlier, most girls would have been head-over-heels with the fact that he was giving them a compliment, ogling over him perhaps. But not me. More reason for him to try harder to win me over. I had this boy, who was from one of the most prominent families in New England, wrapped around my finger. For a moment, I was quite pleased with myself. But only for a moment. The truth was: he was out of my league. I was not like him; I had no desire to be like him. His group was not better, just different; a clique I never had wanted to join—not when I was a young girl at the yacht club, not now, not ever.

He was forthright that he liked the way I looked though, and continued, "You look beautiful," he said, eyeing me up from head to toe.

It wasn't the same way Will (*no, no, no, Katie!*) had looked at me any time he'd thought the same, nor said in the same tone, but I got the point: a guy found me attractive. However, it did make me feel a little like a piece of meat how he looked at me. At any rate, I was hoping the party tonight would get my mind off everything I'd left back home. Unfortunately, the party was short lived.

About an hour into the festivities and amongst a flight of old mahogany stairs, and tall walls with old dark green wallpaper etched with pheasants, Skipper stopped in the foyer and promptly vomited all over an antique oriental rug. Apparently, she'd been taking shots of tequila with her new "boyfriends" [yes two, not just one]. She was the head hen, enjoying that she had two men following her all over. But the alcohol from earlier in the day, and the recent extras, had caught up with the poor girl and she just couldn't hold it in any longer. I gasped wide-eyed, and Brigg snickered a little with his hand over his mouth. I was more worried he'd be angry about the expensive carpet getting soiled, but he genuinely seemed more intent on helping her up and getting her back to our dorm safely. I guess I was wrong in assuming he was nothing but a selfish rich boy and good eye candy. Maybe he had a heart after all.

Across campus, we steadied her. When she seemed too wobbly near the end, he carried her through the rest of the way. Back at our dorm, and once we had her stable and comfortable enough in her bed, I was able to fully look around our room for the first time. Skipper had arrived earlier, on move-in day, and had decorated, of course, and I could now see it. Even in a dim light from a desk lamp, it was sparkle central. Glitter, fluff, and all the girlishness you could imagine. I slapped my forehead. Brigg laughed at the sight as well but then asked concerned, "Think she'll be okay?" He said it almost assuming she and I were old friends and I knew her personally enough to know how her body operated. Without having to answer, she did it for me, grumbling.

"I'm fine. Trust me; I think I got it all out," she mumbled. "Go ahead. Leave me," she finished, sending us on our way with a wave like that of a dismissive queen.

We both laughed. Brigg turned off the desk lamp, then we closed the door and walked back out of the dorm to the street.

He looked at me mannerly, "Hey, you wanna take a walk? No drinks, no party, no people; just us. Yeah?"

I looked back smiling, "Yeah."

He nudged my shoulder and we wandered a bit. The nights sure were chilly, even in early autumn, and—with only my jumpsuit on—I felt cold to the bone. When he saw me shiver, he immediately peeled off his outermost layer, a monogrammed sweater, and helped me put it on. It was a sweet gesture. I did like him, I was attracted to him, but if anything he was just a nice distraction.

We were walking side by side, just enjoying the foggy harbor night, when he stopped abruptly.

"Stay here." He shook his head in saddened disappointment and wandered off nearby onto one of the wharf docks. I was a bit confused.

I saw him approach an older man with a scraggly beard, who was walking barefoot and unsteadily and pulling a wagon. Clearly, the man had been drinking, but he also looked lost on all levels of life. I figured he was down on his luck, and he must have been cold down near the wind coming off the water, too. The man had just sat down on a bench in the fog underneath a streetlight, when Brigg approached him. I was too far away to be a part of the conversation, but Brigg's actions moved me more than his words possibly could have anyway. He put his hand on the older man's shoulder, took off his own shoes, and bent down to put them on the elderly man's feet. It was so touching; I couldn't take my eyes off what was happening. He laid the old fellow down on the bench and tucked him under a few blankets that he took out of the wagon. Then he left him be.

When he returned by my side, he spoke caringly. "Poor guy," he said. "I've seen him out here all season. Never wants any money, only a cup of coffee from time to time. Never wants to sleep on our boat either. I always tell him he's welcome, but he says he likes to wake up to the sun shining off the water."

I thought back to a time on island when the water was sparkling when we… *no! I am not going to think of him!*

The last words Brigg spoke only hit me for a second because my mind was still trying to process the affection he'd just shown another man. He was respectful, and he'd given the man his privacy and pride, and then just let him be. I suppose that was the moment I was sucked in a little more. Brigg wasn't a preppy jerk. Heck, he'd just tucked in *two* needy people for the night!

The air got a little chillier when the wind picked up, so Brigg suggested we go back to the campus library, which was open twenty-four hours a day, seven days a week, and just chat a bit. But first, we needed to swing by the boat, which was at the end of another street, so he could grab a new pair of shoes. I felt safe enough with Brigg at this point, so we made the short trip to the boat on a nearby dock, and then back passed the frat house. We could hear the party from the street, and Brigg noted, "Hope no one does naked cannonballs into the harbor this time."

He said it so matter-of-factly, that I assumed right away he was serious.

Then he laughed, "Joking. Besides, no one streaks around here but me." He nudged me, and I knew he was still joking. I enjoyed his effort to lighten the mood. I think he was trying to show me a different side of him. I'd seen his tailored side, but tonight he was softer.

When we made it to the old library of our private, historic, waterfront school (which I still couldn't believe I'd ended up at), we took a seat, and I took a gander. It was the first time I'd been in the library, and it was magnificent. Somehow, it reminded me of the frat house where Brigg lived: huge wooden beams, a staircase leading to a second floor with an open two-level foyer, and giant antique chandelier. I was proud of myself at that moment to have made it into such a prestigious school. I wasn't really a part of the lifestyle that came with it, but somehow, I was accepted all the same.

Brigg and I chatted for hours, well into those of the wee morning. Right then and there, in the back of my mind—while he talked about grand trips he'd taken and worldly adventures he'd been on—I let myself get lost in his handsome face and tried to move forward from my old life. I wasn't forgetting it; I was just trying to make the best of the direction it had taken.

The next morning, he took me for a sail, and that sealed the deal. He was like me: a salty soul. We understood each other, at least on that level. We went on more dates, and he eventually won me over, and we started dating exclusively. He and Skipper had introduced me to a very social life, too. Skipper had at first dubbed Brigg my "Boy Toy." But he really had become more than that. He wasn't so bad after all; not that I ever thought he was—but he just wasn't as selfish as many would assume if having judged him on his attire and airs alone. He wasn't the love of my life, but it was a nice relationship we had.

A year passed, and I'd become close with Brigg, and even closer with Skipper. I imagined she was everything Kitty had wanted to be: rich beyond belief, glamorous, and loaded with attention because people actually thought she was kind, not because people were afraid of her. As affluent and whimsical as she was, she had a big heart too, and truly listened when we had deep conversations. Of course, many of her conversations ended revolving around wild parties in tropical destinations—which she insisted she'd take me on someday. I always had to laugh. No matter someone's love for luxury (or in my case—lack thereof), if she liked you—she liked you. That simple.

At the end of the school year, I felt like a different person. I still had my past, but I had become part of a new crowd and new life too. I hadn't changed much, other than a few times being "primped up" by Skipper (as she so fondly referred to styling me) for dates. I refused to wear make-up, I ran from hair spray (it made me gag), and I still rejected painting my nails. "Maybe one day," I always promised her. She thought I was full of nonsense, and she kept trying every now and then. She did have a good sense of style though, and I didn't mind her picking out outfits. Narby certainly thought I looked nice when she came to visit. For a moment, I thought maybe she was paying Skipper to style me!

Once freshman year officially ended, Skipper insisted we get our own apartment. The dorms were much to "rustic" for her taste (in better words: a little too small to accommodate her wardrobe), so that was that. We found a place on the water. A little out of my price range, but she insisted she wanted to pay anything above and beyond my budget. We *just had to* live there, she pried. I was fine with it, and extremely grateful. It was a small place, with two bedrooms, a shared bath, and a beautiful, shared living space with a view much like that of the restaurant. At least, I'd have my own room and could avoid all the feathers and frill from her décor this time 'round. It made me sneeze. Now, the bathroom sharing; that'd be an entirely different issue.

I was glad to have bonded so closely with her over the past year, and grateful she had taken me in—especially being that she knew so many people all over town. My connections weren't deeply rooted yet, but I hoped one day to feel as much a part of the community as Skipper by the time I graduated. *Heck, I might even stay here forever,* I thought. For the time being, I was on to see a few other places and move forward: on this occasion, it was off to Brigg's family's house up in Maine for their upcoming annual Fourth of July picnic. Of course, I'd learned that "picnic" in his world meant party, and this one would be none to disappoint.

Chapter 17:

NORTH

There is a certain etiquette that becomes ingrained when hanging around socialites. If even not desiring to be like them, it tends to rub off here and there. I never felt out of the circle, nor a part of it. I knew the right words, the right mannerisms, and had the class. Perhaps it was my own style, and I just added to the group's character. Just because I was a simple girl didn't mean I lacked manners or intelligence. Not to mention, I had the know-how of a sailor. It really was a sport for the rich, so it allowed me easy entrance to the clique whether I asked for it or not. I remembered back to childhood, and how Kitty's clique had been a border of which not to cross for others of the opposite ilk. I recollected this deeply, and it kept me humble. I never wanted anyone I met to think of me as prissy, or above them. Then, I would be just like Kitty. I imagined briefly what Kitty's child would grow up to be like. *Will's child.* I immediately shut the thought down so I wouldn't get sick again and threw it in my internal vault.

Once Skipper and I had moved in and unpacked in the apartment after freshman year, it seemed we were packing right back up again for the long weekend even further north in Maine, for Brigg's family's event. It was easy to load everything from our waterfront pad right down to the docks since we'd be taking the yacht. Just like the end of last summer, Skipper's butler had reemerged to help us load the bags on the boat anyway. It seemed to allow a bunch of abled young yachtie men—our own "boyfriends"—an easy out from easy labor. They must have been paying this soul good money to do such simple work.

I loved being on Brigg's boat. Sailing north on this day was relaxing. The current was from the south, and the heavy breeze from the southeast was enough to pull us along for the half-day long journey. Of course, the boat came complete with a full captain and crew, so really it was a day for Brigg and his boys (two of whom Skipper seemed to own at this point) and us girls to reminisce about the school year past, and plan more future fun. And the fun would come soon enough. I would learn all too quickly that fun was part of this new life, and the full intro to Brigg's world and his family, was just up the coast.

Pulling up to the private dock at Brigg's family's compound brought me the same feeling when walking up to the frat house for the first time: *someone is trying to impress everyone*. As always, I was not enthralled with the lifestyles of the wealthy, but I did have to stop and stare for a moment. The property was sprawling, and from the angle in which we'd pulled up along the pilings, it was downright colossal. I'd been told it was a "cottage," but I thought at that moment that perhaps they'd been referring to the guest house. Noticing our arrival, a gardener tending to some old English boxwoods, signaled to a lady that we'd arrived. She hurried into the main house, and then came back out again with some welcome drinks. We met her on the dock.

"Oh Brigg, look at you," she hollered from the dock as we unloaded and stepped off the boat. She was warm and took him in her arms after putting a tray down on a little iron end table, which was part of an entire set-up.

"Nanny, I've missed you," he said and hugged her back. "Please meet my girlfriend, Kate."

Girlfriend. It was official, and it had been said out loud. No going back now. So much for carving my future alone.

"So nice to meet you," I said as I extended my hand, but she pulled me in just as she had with Brigg and gave me a warm hug.

"Let me go get your parents. They've been counting down the hours 'til you'd get here!" she squealed with delight.

As "Nanny" wandered off, I wondered if she was, in fact, a caretaker, or if that was her name. Brigg's following comment explained.

"She took care of my brother's and me growing up. My mom was so busy working, so she often made us meals, cleaned up after us, and bustled us around."

I recalled Narby being the same sort of caregiver. But throughout follow-up commentary, I realized "involved" in my childhood, and "involved" in his meant two very different things. My parents had worked hard, and truly needed the help. As it turned out, Brigg's mother didn't work, but she didn't stay home to raise her kids either. Spa days, hiring various amounts of helpers, charity events, poolside luncheons with her friends, and shopping outings were her "work."

"Briggy!" announced a long-legged, chin-length bleach blond-haired woman in a shift dress. I recognized the same fabric pattern from the store Skipper had dragged me to back near school.

"Momsy!" he said and held out his arms to welcome the woman from whom he clearly got his height.

"Mother, I'd like you to meet Kate."

"Well, finally! Look at how darling you are," she said as she took my shoulders and took me in, much like Skipper had, to give me the once-over when we'd met. *Must be a New England thing*, I thought. *Europeans like the double cheek kisses; New Englanders like the double shoulder grip*. I made a mental note.

"Thanks! You're just as beautiful as Brigg told me," I complimented. She really was. Imagining she was at least three decades our senior since Brigg had mentioned he was the youngest of the three boys, she really didn't have a line on her skin. It was weird to me that her delighted voice, didn't match the expression on her face though, like her skin was somehow attached to an internal electric dog fence, preventing her smile lines from escaping. I had to shut down my thoughts and remind myself of my manners before I giggled out loud to the horror of plastic surgery.

"Nanny, please bring those drinks right this way!" his mom ordered, seeming a bit snappy.

The respective Nanny (*did she have a real name?*) returned to the iron table to pick the tray back up and bring us mimosas. The crew stayed busy tying up the boat (*oh dear, please do it the right way this time*, I laughed internally), and the passengers—me included, of course—accepted the cocktails with thanks. With that, Brigg's mom "Missy" hurried us off on our way to have snacks. Her name worried me a bit. "Kitty" had been like a real cat. Was Missy going to be prissy? Goodness, I hoped not. Again, I reminded myself to be open and not judge others. So far, this elite class had been nothing short of welcoming and kind, so shame on me for thinking otherwise.

We'd been directed to a patio by Nanny, and when I sat down, I was able to peer around a bit. Up close—real close—the cottage was castle-esque. It appeared an old field stone farmhouse that had been added to over the years, somehow keeping in mind the era of the structure and seeming to match each stone flawlessly. The end results of the additions—a flowing, three-story mansion with multiple chimneys, patios, and entertaining setups. A stream hugged a corner of the house, and made off onto the property and past an old bank barn. The boathouse matched the home, as did the guest house. Period structures sat here and there: an old outhouse was decorated with baskets full of fresh flowers around the bottom, and a wishing well with the date of the property etched into the rim. I imagined neither was still in use. Who needed an outhouse and hard-earned water when you probably had a marble bathroom and filtered water from some pure spring!

About an hour later after another mimosa and some "nibblies" (which Missy had referred to snacks), we got the grand tour. My imagery of marble and magic water was confirmed. The room in which I was to stay was a suite with marble tile, alright, also: a crystal chandelier, button-pinched satin pillows, a beautiful soft rug (sadly made of alpaca skins), and little golden starfish in the windows. I thought it funny that his mother referred to each room as a "quarter" as we walked around. I guess they really were sailors to their core. Walking down another hall in the first level of the home gave way to a hint of cigar smoke creeping through the air. Following, a few emphatic chuckles came from men behind some old pocket-sliding, maple doors. We arrived, and Missy pushed them aside to reveal our little gaggle complete with me, Brigg, Skipper, and a few other guys from school, with Nanny following behind.

"Come in, crew!" A man very much resembling Brigg held out his arms just as warmly as his mother and Nanny had, again noting the seaside terminology. It was nice to see they were a tight knit family as I'd been with my parents. I wondered if my folks would have been proud of me to have seemingly joined such a crowd, if not just for the fact that they were hospitable, loving, and nautical.

Brigg shook his father's hand firmly, and they leaned in for a hug just as wholeheartedly as their laughter. The same gestures followed from the other two men standing by Brigg's dad. I assumed they were the two elder brothers. Heck, they could have been triplets with Brigg!

Even more endearingly than the first time Brigg had extended his hand to mine a year ago, his father smiled, shaking his head. "Well, aren't you everything my son has been talking about?" he said and then he took my hand and kissed it, still covering my hand with both of his own when he was done, seeming to take me in for a moment. I had no idea Brigg had even spoken much about me to his family, so it was a pleasant surprise.

The same sort of gestures and words came from his brothers and intros were made all around. Skipper and Missy were in their own little world, filling each other in on New England trendsetter gossip, and whom they shared as mutual friends. I couldn't tell if their laughs were genuine, or to see who could out fake the other. *Weird little song and dance*, I thought. I made more mental notes.

"Well, now, let's not waste a beautiful day in the library. Back outside we go," said his dad and shuffled us in a funny and hurried little manner, over-exaggerating at the same time. I liked their being candid and relaxed, and it made me feel the same.

We returned to the patio, and a few kids were now swinging from a tire swing in bright white pants and light blue oxford tops off in the yard. A voice from somewhere in a garden followed, "Boys, please don't get yourselves dirty. At least stay clean for the picnic!" This was Brigg's oldest brother's wife, and the brother rolled his eyes at the comment. It made me laugh though when, less than fifteen minutes later, the brother was scolding his kids to keep their boat shoes from getting grass stains. My childhood had been filled with those very stains, dirty pants, and—if I'd had a tire swing as well—I'd probably have had a permanent black stain on my trousers. I kept these thoughts to myself though. They were my memories to cherish and not to be used as judgment against others.

As we sat for another hour or so, a big white tent that workers had been assembling all day was now being set up with tables, chairs, and red, white, and blue décor all over. It was about as fancy Americana as one could imagine, and I was curious as to why such a large tent was present when there were only about a dozen of us. Of course, another hour later, when guests arrived by boats, elaborate cars, chauffeurs, and even a seaplane, my question was explained. Brigg hadn't mentioned the entire town was invited! Turns out, none of the people were from town, of course. Every guest owned other regal houses along the coast, but their main homes were mostly in the superior sections of big cities.

If the display of wealth wasn't overwhelming enough, the food spread surely was. Before long, lobsters were steaming in pots, oysters were being shucked, and champagne was being served on trays by white-gloved men. The hosts made mentions that they'd added a little "rustic touch" to the holiday this year: making note of the cornbread, chicken wings, and other simpler American fare. If chicken wings were rustic, then what did that make a girl like me who ate them? A few kids ran wildly from their baby-sitters: breaking free to dig into the food. I was pleased that the first grab was at the wings. One of the fathers followed suit, and I was just delighted. However, my glee was soon shut down when the man began to partake in the chicken wing eating with a fork and knife. *Fork and knife!* Will would have been covered in sauce, licking his fingers. *Will.* This was clearly getting too hard. My emotional efforts to lock him away were not functioning correctly.

I cut short the memories of my "old life." Not that I was part of a new one, but I at least wanted to enjoy a day without painful reflection. After some eating, drinking, and meeting new folks, Brigg, his friends, and a few cousins went to play croquet, and I excused myself to wander the grounds. I found myself back at the water's edge. The salty breeze was mixed with the scent of the boxwoods I'd noticed upon arrival: earthy, stale, yet somehow alive. The bushes were perfectly shape by a gardener who had seemed to disappear when the guests had arrived. Back home, all would have been welcome: no matter the class. It made me feel a little alien again. For a moment, I was taken back to the time at the carnival when I'd walked away, feeling like I'd never fit in. Here I was again: amongst a type of people I just didn't quite understand. I had more in common with the nanny and groundskeeper: hard-working, modest, excepting. How I had let myself get sucked in became an unnerving question now starting to stir in my head. But before I could let my thoughts consume me, I pulled myself together. I wasn't a child running from a fair anymore. I was grown, I had moved on, and I was accepted. Before I could second-guess myself, I wandered back to the festivities, instead of walking away.

Skipper was drunk, as were many others. Alcohol seemed to be the norm with this unit. Kids were trampling plants with no respect as their mothers looked on—assuming a landscaper would just fix or replace them the next day, and the fathers looked like geese: all squawk-ing amongst themselves with drinks and cigars in their hands, and laughing up to the sky as if to see who had the longest neck. The sun was setting, and the noise of the gaggle only seemed to get louder as it got darker. Of course, the lavish landscape-lighting wouldn't let the party stop. This estate was meant for a party: rain or shine, cold or hot, day or night. I just stood there and stared and watched the sun set. Only the sound of genuine laughter made me turn my head. One of the neph-ews from earlier in the day, now along with his little sister I'd not yet met, were running with sparklers across the perfectly trimmed lawn. My mouth parted a bit, and I could feel my heart slow. *The sparklers.* It was like watching a movie of myself—of *us.* The vision was only inter-rupted with a huge bang. Everyone turned toward the bay to watch fire-works that were now going off one after another. Everyone cheered and whistled, drunk and in a world of their own. I couldn't hear anything though. The fireworks seemed blurry. Maybe I hadn't eaten enough. *Where was Brigg?* My mind was every which direction, trying to figure out why I felt so hazy. I tilted my head back for a deep breath, grasping with my nostrils for fresh air, and feeling drowned in a sea of glitz and glam. As I looked up, the thousands of little fireballs from the explo-sives remained blurry, so I turned away from the direction everyone else looked. However, I was unable to escape the lights in the sky. As I made my way to the empty tire swing next to a pond away from the docks and chaos, I saw a sparkle of a reflection in the water. I looked up into the sky and noticed a single shooting star. For a moment, I felt like I was lying on my back in a fallow field, in a place I belonged.

Chapter 18:

THE BLINDSIDE

The rest of college passed quickly as I dated Brigg and rented the apartment with Skipper. Narby visited often and didn't question why I wasn't reciprocal with the visits home. She understood my hardened stance on returns to where things had ended so poorly, so abruptly. My childhood had come to a screeching halt those many years ago, and I was fast to pick up and move on. It was a chance to truly grow up. Yes, I missed those good ol' days, but this gave me an opportunity to refine myself, focus on the future, and possibly move on as well. No matter the circumstance, Narby and my New England crew were steadfastly proud of me, and it kept my head held high, and not wallowing in in memory, or even regret. I'm sure old island friends and even friends from back in the Pines were proud of me, too. One day, I'd find out, but this was not the time. I hadn't fully moved on yet. From time to time, I seemed to find that very regret sneaking around, second-guessing myself about if I'd reacted too soon that day that I'd shut Will out. But I had a new life, new friends, and a boyfriend. I never thought my best friend and boyfriend would be from such a different walk of life than me, but they respected me, they took care of me, and we were close, nonetheless.

By the time college ended, it was only natural Skipper and I had a joint graduation party. It was to be at the very restaurant we'd had our first "girlfriend date," and her parents had gone over the top with décor and planning and even rented out the entire place. I'd gotten to know them over the years and learned where she got her flare for all things grand and glam. They truly did go all out: a banquet of all New England cuisine possible, and all the top shelf liquor they could smash into one bar area. The wine, cheese, and hors d'oeuvres were just as flashy as the people (Narby was present too of course) who walked around nibbling at them, and the champagne fountain was quite the sight. Alcohol wasn't something considered with people of this circle. It was just another piece of their preppy puzzle—often hard to figure out, but after a few drinks, easily understood. People were people, no matter the class. Even though some noses sniffed the air a little higher, we were all sniffing the same air. Just, these people assumed these appurtenances came with their life, like a side dish. Second homes, nannies, gardeners, bourbon, were all just naturally a part of their world. I didn't judge. They never judged me, so why should I?

A few hours into the party, people were sozzled, dancing, and causing the haughty scene they lived for. I'd gotten used to it, but being accustomed now to this way of life, didn't mean I wanted to be a part of it forever. I knew Skipper was a forever friend, but the thought of me spending my life with Brigg—as Skipper had randomly suggested in a few [maybe too many!] conversations—was stifling. I'd never put much thought into what would happen beyond college. *Had I really been selfish enough to use Brigg for four years just to keep my mind off Will?* No, I hadn't. It wasn't in me to be that selfish. But I wondered then: why had I never gotten more serious with him besides thinking we'd always just date?

Songs at our party had jumped from one to the next, but there came a point, the music stopped abruptly. It seemed unnatural then how people seemed to exit the dance floor at the same time. Something must have been wrong, so I turned around with them to see what was going on, but then I heard a voice come over the microphone. It was Brigg. I noticed then no one standing between us, but everyone was looking at us from around the edges of the dance floor. I immediately felt nervous, fearful, and like a bad joke was about to be played on me.

"Kate, four years is a darn long time to be together," he said. In the background, a man drunkenly and loudly mumbled (regarding his own marriage), "Thirty is a heck of a lot longer son." The man seemed more agitated than proud of being in such a long relationship. Everyone laughed. I was still clueless and tuned my hearing back toward Brigg.

He continued, "I may have taken a while to realize this, but you are a good woman to spend the rest of my time in this world with. Marry me?" It seemed like a half-done proposal; like I was good "enough." Will loved me from the second he had met me, and… *no, no… Will is not going to mess this up.* However, I still didn't know what "this" even was. *What was happening?*

Out from a little aqua box, Brigg pulled a ring. The diamond was huge, and those that edged it sparkled blindingly. I recognized the type of ring as those his mother and her friends wore. I felt so unimportant, so ordinary. He put it on me, and I immediately felt claustrophobic; like an anchor was weighing me down. It was not a good anchor. Not the anchored feeling of being safely harbored. No. This was like a ball and chain in a prison. It was supposed to be a happy moment, but I felt sick. Perhaps I needed to suck it up, and just let it be what it was; go for the ride. I finally got the nerve to make eye contact with Narby, and she just kept staring at me, as if she were the one waiting for me to answer the proposal. I just shrugged and tried to smile. She did the same in return. The fact was everyone around us was happy. No one was jealous or unhappy for us. Everyone seemed genuinely filled with joy for our new level of commitment. Maybe they weren't my crowd of people, but I seemed to be theirs. They were sincerely joyous.

Only wanting more strongly than ever to get Will's face out of my head, I smiled. But before I could say anything at all—shouting, toasts, and hugs ensued from all angles. *What had I just done?* Narby's expression of utter shock confirmed my own feelings, but Skipper's splendor was enough to trump any negative crux in the air.

The next announcement blindsided me even more.

As the cheering quieted, Brigg silenced it completely with a loud tap of his champagne glass.

"Oh, it's not over yet. Now, you all know me—I love to keep the surprises going." He then looked at me, right in my face; the big brown eyes that lured a lady in and made her a slave to his charm. Then, he said, "We're moving!"

I just raised my eyebrows and widened my eyes, standing stiff as a board.

I thought it was time I said something, if not at least to acknowledge I was a part of my own little engagement, "We are?" I was nervous. Thank goodness drunk people didn't take notice to emotion much. And once again, the cheering began.

Apparently, Brigg felt it more necessary to explain to the crowd than his fiancé (*fiancé?*) about the plans he had made without me. Looking around, he was proud to let everyone know, "I've become a partner with my father and brothers, and we'll be opening a new resort out west: an all-season lodge and resort with golf, tennis, a spa, skiing, restaurants, and beautiful grounds!" He spoke about these grand plans with more pride he'd even put into his proposal. By this time, he'd dropped my hand, and was waving his arms around enthusiastically explaining the details of the new project and wandered off into the crowd. He finally shared our new address, and I almost fainted. I was to move over two-thousand miles west: away from everything and everyone I'd ever known. The engagement was one thing; maybe I should have even expected it. But this—moving so far, and so far from saltwater—was dizzying. My head was spinning. I excused myself to go to the wharf walk for some fresh air, but more so because I thought I'd throw up.

I must have looked like a woman in childbirth labor with my intense breathing trying to keep from blacking out. Maybe I even appeared someone hyperventilating. If it had not been for Narby scurrying right down after me with a glass of water, I may have fallen into the harbor.

She was thoughtful for a moment before she spoke, allowing me both time to swallow some water and think long and hard about which words to say before she said them out loud.

"That was a lot. Unexpected." She was serious, concerned, and low speaking. I knew her words came from a place of worry for me *and* herself. If I was moving for good, then what family would she have left?

It took me a moment, since the only words I'd spoken between hoots and hollers were few, and stark.

"Yeah. I… I didn't know what to say." I kept looking out into the harbor, too shamed to make eyes with her, but also to keep from breaking down.

You do have a lot of memories with Brigg, but you also have a lot of memories with…" Her voice trailing off was enough to let me know exactly whom she was thinking of and where this conversation was about to go. I don't know what go into me at that moment, but it made the hair on my neck stand up, and I became defensive. I turned to Narby and looked her straight in the eyes.

"You know, he didn't define me! That is the past. You keep hanging on to hope that I'll reconnect with him, but I won't!" I instantly felt terrible for snapping. I looked at her now, crying, and there was no need for me to explain anymore. It was an unspoken apology from me, but, more so, an understanding on so many levels from Narby. She had to turn her head while she rubbed my back with one hand, to keep herself from crying. She knew the last hour had been an end to any hope that she had held on to for so long—the hope that I would come home and maybe get back together with Will. She nodded her head. I continued, still sobbing.

"Brigg is good to me. He has never hurt me. Will did: twice. Brigg's family has become an extension of my own." So had Will's, and I knew everything else coming out of my mouth was merely grasping at straws to find fault with Will. Narby kept looking like she had more to say but didn't know how, like there was something about Will she was hiding, but not her right to share. As we heard Brigg continuing from up on the deck, ranting and raving with his impressive plans, I continued giving my own speech. Narby knew I wasn't trying to convince her. She knew, as well as I did, that I was trying to convince myself. I reminded her about all the times she and I had spent at Brigg's home in Maine, and all the holidays we'd shared as well. I reminded her that she had always been included, and that she always would be. I told her how Brigg had always been a gentleman. I went on and on and probably would have until I'd exhausted myself, but then Skipper found us.

"Ladies! Where have you been? Kate, this is your night!" She took each of our hands and pulled us with a pouting mouth back toward the party. She led the way, and as we were forced to walk single file back up the wharf ramp, Narby was in between us and turned back to look at me and stop for a second.

Narby said, "I believe you. When it's time to move on, it's just time." She gave me a quick squeeze on my hand, a smile, and turned up to keep walking. A worried look came over my face, and I couldn't see it but it was on hers too. She wanted to believe me. I wanted to believe myself. But "*want*" was different than "*did.*" For now, I could only hope.

As we walked back into the festivities, the men were heavy into the whiskey and cigars, and the ladies were gossiping about this and that. Kids were running wild, and the whole point of the party—our graduation—had been completely forgotten. Perhaps Skipper thought my saddened look came from the afterthought, so she had a toast of her own to make. She grabbed two glasses of champagne, handed me one, and put her arm around my shoulder, grabbed a microphone and silenced everyone. *If anyone thought Brigg had a way of catching attention, then they hadn't seen Skipper in action!* She gave a speech to share some funny memories, but even greater, to show what true friends we were. People cheered again. At this, Narby and I truly had something to smile about, and temporarily freed us of any negative thoughts. Skipper took me aside once the cheering settled again and became serious. It was unlike her to be so deep in thought, or at least for more than ten minutes, but we went to the edge of the dock, sat down, linked arms, and had a heart-to-heart that lasted almost an hour. She told me she knew what it was like to be unsure of the future. She told me she'd bounced around from school to school as a child, as they moved from one wealthy town to the next following her dad's job. She managed to make me aware she was okay after each move. Maybe she was trying to convince herself, just as I had with Narby an hour or so earlier, but all she was saying wasn't sinking in. All I wondered then was if the plans I'd made for myself my entire life, and my own dreams, would now be controlled by someone else.

At the party's end, I found out the big move would be in less than a month. *Blindside number three.* When I was made aware of this news, I was so exhausted at that point, that I just didn't care anymore. I figured: *Why not? Why not just up and go, and give it a shot?* College had treated me well, and I'd come here blindly too. How could moving west be any different? But it was: it was to be much, much different.

Chapter 19:

WEST

Old money was something I'd become accustomed to accepting for the past four years, but the nouveau riche were an entirely different class, more so because they lacked it entirely. As soon as we pulled into our gated community sitting next to the resort-to-be and—still with a few lots left for sale—there seemed a flatness in the air. Mailboxes matched, landscaping matched, and cars were all black. Nothing was original and unique; nothing was special. Just like my engagement ring, it all seemed ostentatious and similar. Maybe my ring was—in fact—my key to this obnoxious club. It was nothing but tasteless and showy. As we drove slowly around the neighborhood, up and down hills and around bends (both of which I wasn't used to, since being from such a flat state), it felt cold, too—huge brick homes with no life moving around outside. Even in summer, the place had a chill in the air and unwelcoming feel to it. I couldn't quite wrap my head around how people could have such vast and beautifully manicured properties, and not use them. Like I had in the past, I was determined not to be judgmental though, and give them all a chance (whoever "them" would be), whether they were like me or not. At least, they were worth a chance. However, something in my gut told me, this was going to be a heck of a struggle in my new home: the people, the lifestyle, and the distance from everything I knew and loved.

Skipper promised to visit often and Narby as frequently as she could too; besides, I had Brigg. We would do this together.

There was something reminiscent of these homes, how they mimicked the appearance of Brigg's family Estate in Maine. But that was just it: a mimic, a façade. There were no true bones or history behind these homes. People didn't appreciate the detail of what surrounded them. "The bigger the better; the more expensive the better" seemed to be screaming out each window; windows furnished with expensive drapes, of course. If the outside of these homes spoke volumes of the sort of people who resided in them, then I was worried I would be the black sheep right away. The first neighbor I met lived across the street, and her visit certainly didn't make me feel part of the pasture.

Brigg had headed out to his future-resort grounds to meet with a client of his, and I stayed at the house to unpack a few things. I wore a little pair of gym shorts and a long-sleeved tee shirt I'd picked up at an old lobster wharf in Maine. My hair was up in a wild mess of a bun on top of my head. The windows had been cracked to let out the smell of new carpet and paint, and in came the sound of tiny, trotting deer hooves. But the scent that blew in as well threw me off. *Did the wildlife wear perfume around here?*

My thoughts of ungulates dissipated when our doorbell rang. It was the first time I heard it and it echoed loudly through our two-flight staircase foyer, startling me. I opened the door to find a slight woman, with high heels, a tennis skirt, a tight-fitting and low-cut thin sweater, all brightly colored with wild patterns, but somehow all still matching. Her hair was shaped into a big wig-looking sort of blond tower, and her make-up looked spray-painted on. Before I had a chance to say hello, she spoke.

"Hi! I'm Candy!" she greeted me, practically sticking her hand in my face, and kept rambling like a programed robot. "I live right there across the street." Her gestures were almost robotic as well, as she made her points with little daintily cupped hands, "Are you the maid?"

I looked wide-eyed at her and almost felt bad that she'd clearly been sucked into a world of such one-level rigidity, that she seemed only to want to acknowledge—or continue her efforts with—anyone "above" a cleaning lady.

I replied, "No, I own the house." My answer was a bit of a stretch, as I really had no idea what legal documents my name was even on. I'd up and moved. No questions asked, I just tagged along.

"Oh goodness! I'm so terribly sorry. I just thought since…" she trailed off, looking over my outfit [lacking in any quality or brand name of course]. "… well, you just looked… busy."

Nice save lady.

The emotional face slap I gave her with a simple eyebrow lift felt a little nice; almost like the time I'd slipped a wet rubber frog down Kitty's back. *Score one for me! Oh gosh, was this really to become a game?* I thought. Well, at least I'd need some entertainment in this place that was turning out to be drab already.

I spoke again "No worries," I said and tried to squeeze out a smile, hiding my instant desire to shut the door in her face. I cocked my head and stayed silent, as if to leave her to finish what she'd come for and show her I just wanted her to wrap up her rant.

She picked up where she'd left off before the back-handed insult, "Anyway, I baked these up for you, and here's some champs to go with it." *Champs?* She lifted a large bottle of expensive bubbly from the porch floor and served a little gold-rimmed dish of cookies like a waitress. It was a kind gesture at least, and I accepted it with thanks.

Again, she continued mechanically. "Is your husband home?" It was said so directly, and in a needy manner, that I was a bit perplexed.

I wasn't sure how to answer, so I replied, "Umm, well, he's out right now, but…" As I was about to finish, Brigg pulled back in. It seemed he'd forgotten something. He also seemed not to have noticed us on the porch. That much was clear when he went in and out of the house, only to hop back in his luxury sports car again. But before he could drive away, Candy was off back down the front walk in his direction, waving a hand in the air flirtatiously, much resembling someone bidding at auction. I was left standing with a bottle of booze and cookies.

I figured I'd follow along and try to give Brigg warning before she blabbered him to death too, but it was too late. Even before he got back out of his car to be polite, she was chatting his ear off.

"Well, hello," her voice was softer, cuter, and even vulnerable. It was desperate. "I'm Candy, and I live just across the street. My husband is on business trips a lot, so feel free to stop by any time." Her eyes became dreamy almost when she spoke the word "*any.*" I couldn't help but wonder if they were swingers or something, or perhaps she really *was* just prepositioning my fiancé right in front of me. *Shameless.*

I fully prepared for Brigg to reply, but all he could get out was, "Thanks?"

She smiled with a little flash of her faux eyelashes, walked away deer-trotting back down our driveway just like she'd arrived, and off on the short walk back to her own house.

Brigg looked at me, I shrugged my shoulders, and he came over to give me a kiss on the head before shaking his head and getting back in his car to drive off. "Love you, babe."

"You too," I replied. But it felt sour. I'd never quite gotten accustomed to saying "I love you" even after four years of being together. It felt unnatural, forced, and I suppose I just said it out of habit. I was beginning to feel like a robot myself. Four years really *had* changed me. I was following someone else's path and not my own; I was wearing jewelry that cost enough to buy a farm back home; and I was muted and on auto-play. To forget my past—which I knew was unhealthy—I just went along with everything these days. Although I'd never actually said yes to marrying Brigg, I'd gone along with a move far west (which was as good of a "yes," I supposed), and now I stood with pricey alcohol and a dropped jaw knowing my new neighbors reminded me of a certain movie with machine-like cloned wives. *What was I becoming?*

The notion of my thoughts left me lightly reeling, so I wandered aimlessly back into the house. It was just a massive empty space now, as the movers hadn't arrived yet. We hadn't packed much since we'd only brought things from our respective residences at school, but his parents had insisted on fully furnishing our home as an early wedding present. *Wedding? Yikes! I wasn't ready for that thought.* On that note, I became downright nauseous, put the champagne and treats down, and walked out the back door for some fresh air. I hadn't quite adjusted to the altitude, so perhaps my nausea and headache that started to creep in was just sickness from the newness of the place. But the thought of a wedding had really hit me. It weighed heavy in my heart, my mind, but especially—on my hand. I looked down on my finger. The hands around here fit with the rocks that held them: manicured, soft, not a single wrinkle. But my hands were proud: a few lines that were memories from my past. Just like saltwater was in my veins, so was being simple. I didn't need someone else to cut my own nails. It would feel invasive, and downright embarrassing. *Were people incapable of simple hygiene?* The thoughts that kept running through my head were very trivial as I stared at the gigantic diamond. It was baffling that the things I now had to avoid were based on vanity, and not deep-rooted emotion like the things I had run from back home; things that were real and soulful. There seemed no depth around here other than the mountain valleys. The woman at my front door wouldn't be a friend; there were no corn fields, no familiar faces, and no saltwater; and the only water was that which I looked over at that very minute – a man-made lake in the backyard with a lit dock made of some recycled material to resemble wood. Attractive, yes. Real, no; just like Candy, and Kitty, and maybe even my future mother-in-law. At these thoughts, combined with my longing for home, I felt light-headed. I turned around to grab one of the cookies doll face had brought over, and let it settle in my stomach. Maybe the sugar would give me a little rush. As I chewed, I noticed a little note sticking out under the perfectly stacked pile.

Enjoy your cozy home! ~C

Cozy? This place was huge! And "home?" This did *not* feel like home. Thank goodness the movers arriving distracted me.

"Hey guys!" I said cheerfully and answered the front door once again. (Thank goodness Candy hadn't returned!)

A nice group of men made their welcomes and intros and put me in charge of directing our things. As they went to get the first piece of furniture, I looked around one last time of what the space looked like empty. I had no idea how it would be possible to fill each area of this huge home with things to make it seem "cozy." I liked snug, and this was not snug.

The first item that came through the door made me stagger back. On a stand was a zebra that Brigg's uncles had shot while on safari in Africa. I drew the line at sport hunting and had them put it aside. I planned on having them put it right back in the truck once they unloaded it. Yuck! Brigg's parents had spared no expense, and I knew his mother was behind the interior design; simply because – it was everything I wasn't. Once again, I had sat back to let someone else control what was rightfully my space. I had become a portrait on the wall in my own house and life.

At least I didn't have to give much direction to the movers as per the setup. Brigg's mom had sent an entire lay-out for the men, so I decided just to leave them and go for a walk. At this point, I wouldn't even care if they'd steal anything. I didn't truly think they would. They were hardworking people, like I was used to, and I think they could tell by our short conversation, that I was more like them than the world I lived in. I asked them when they'd be done, and it seemed I had a few hours to myself to wander around. I put the plate of cookies out for the men and told them to help themselves. I figured now was a good time to go explore the preserved space that surrounded the resort and our gated community, so I stuck on a pair of sneakers, drank a glass of water, and began to head out.

Walking back through the house made me loathe what I'd agreed to. I felt bad for being ungrateful almost—but it just wasn't me, and it was entirely my fault. An elevator, a wine cellar, a bowling alley, a cigar bar with a custom humidor, and fanciness everywhere, just pushed me faster to get out of the house. By the time I hit a paved trail at the edge of our yard, I decided to take an equestrian path instead, and started jogging. I had planned on a meandering walk, but I broke into a run, and just kept going.

The fresh air really did make me feel good, and the water I had drank before I left had helped clear my headache as well. Summer out here was different. The sounds, smells, and the views were different. The wildlife and landscapes were breathtaking and new—something to appreciate. I became out of breath a little quicker than usual due to the altitude, I supposed, so I slowed to the originally intended walk. My walk lasted a little longer than expected, and by the time I returned to the house the movers had left.

When I walked in, I was walloped in the head by what the space had become. My home was a combination of the frat house, the Maine "cottage," and with the flair of affluence a feathery-butted game bird might flash. I slapped myself on the forehead with the palm of my hand.

In the short while we'd chatted in the morning, Brigg had reminded me to be ready for the soft-opening reveal of the resort that night. The weather was perfect for it. I headed back to the master bath for a shower, and to get ready for the evening, and just reminded myself to stay humble and grateful.

Entering my room gave way to a display of dresses on the bed. I couldn't imagine he'd come home, dropped them off, and gone out again in the time I'd been gone. But I looked at the clock, and I really had been gone for some time. A few different colors and silhouettes of style were draped over the end of the king-sized bed, and I thought it was a sweet gesture for him to have wanted to charm me. Matching shoes and handbags were set next to the pieces, and I knew at that point he must have gotten help from someone in his efforts to style me. *Maybe Skipper was hiding in a closet.*

After my shower, I tried on a few dresses. None of them were really my style, so by the time I was dressed in the third out of the five, I just settled on it since it fit. At that moment, the phone rang, and I answered to Brigg's voice.

"Well, what did you think?" he asked, clearly wanting to know about the dresses.

"They're beautiful. Thank you," I said and confirmed his need to know he'd done well. I'd become good at lying, and my voice had taken on a flatness I didn't understand anymore. Or maybe it wasn't lying; maybe it was just trying to make the best of my new life without speaking my truth as to avoid conflict and appear to be gracious. Goodness knew I'd had enough conflict in one lifetime, and I just hoped now for a life free of pain. If it meant changing a bit (or a lot), then I was willing. Anything was better than going in reverse and going back to a place where *Will might be... might be sitting on the dock with a kid, Kitty's kid.* The thought almost made me lurch, and I suppose made me become silent too.

"Babe, you okay?" Brigg asked worriedly when I didn't reply to some questions he'd asked and I'd not even heard.

"Oh, yeah, sorry. Zipper got stuck."

Jeez, I really *was* a liar.

He got back on point as if to hurry me along, "Okay, well get ready. I have a car on the way, so you have an hour, my love."

"Got it. I'm getting pretty," I noted. I then looked in the mirror and made a motion of sticking my finger down my throat with my tongue out.

We said our goodbyes and hung up our phones.

I looked in the mirror. The dress, the shoes, nor the bag: none of it was me. Not that dressing up *was* ever me, but this was going too far. Things were too low, too high, too tight, and hugged me in places

166

that seemed too revealing. I felt naked, in a way. But when I got to the party, I realized all the ladies were dressed similarly, so at least I wasn't in the teeniest dress. In fact, I had the most modest dress of all, and that wasn't saying much! All the other women had half-exposed breasts, slits in their dresses to reveal toned and sprayed-tanned thighs, and low-cut backs revealing the same skin tone. I wrinkled my nose wondering how their spouses could possibly want to touch—let alone kiss—people with so much goop on their face and skin. Yuck! *Manners, Katie. Manners.* I put myself in check again.

At the clubhouse, champagne and hors d'oeuvres were being carried around aimlessly by the infamous, white-gloved men who seemed to pop out of walls at any event I attended these days. *Sneaky buggers*, I thought. They reminded me of new fathers navigating a stroller for the first time. I spotted Candy, and she darted at me with a few friends. How they resembled Kitty and her crew set me back for a moment. But at least they seemed kind enough. (Hence: *Enough.*)

Candy waved her hands around like seeing a best friend she hadn't seen in years, "Girls! Meet our new neighbor, Kate!"

I remained myself, and had no intention of giving into the show, nor creating a façade. I was cordial and that was it.

"Nice to meet all of you," I said and nodded. Perhaps it came off too much as an opening to a business meeting, but no one seemed to notice. They went around and around asking me questions: everything from my favorite type of shoes and my favorite place to play tennis, to my favorite drink. None of the former I had any answers to, as I had been hoping for a little more interest as to where I came from, who in my life was important, or what my dreams were. At least we found common ground on education. Well, at least the fact that they somehow [miraculously] graduated college! But they'd all graduated a decade before me. At this, I was shocked. I had assumed they were all younger than they were since they had so few wrinkles and such shallow conversations. Then I realized the lack of lines was from chemicals injected into their expressionless faces. Their lips looked like ducks, and their chests like proud hens how they seemed to bust out of the tops of their dresses. I got lost in their conversations at one point out of boredom, and my mind wandered to a place of anger. I didn't expect this, but as I watched Brigg chat with likely businessmen and new friends on the other side of the room, and next to a model of the future resort—I frowned. I wondered if he planned to inject the same brainwashing poison into my face to make me like these women, these machines. I mentally stuck my finger down my throat again.

Hours passed with senseless conversation, and I became truly tired. A day of moving, adventuring, and meeting this new group of wind-up dolls had exhausted me. I excused myself from the group, said my farewells to Brigg (who seemed not to care I was leaving, but more interested in business), and let the driver take me home. I'd have been completely capable of driving myself home, as Brigg had bought me a new SUV. He had insisted I not buy a truck as I'd intended because an SUV would "handle better" in this area and the new terrain. I think he was just embarrassed to have his future wife be seen in a pickup truck, and so I had what everyone else had: the expensive, black, shiny car with room for seven, screaming "I'm rich!" Our house had six bed-rooms, seven bathrooms, and more bonus rooms than could ever be filled at once, even with a giant family. *Family? If "wedding" hadn't hit me hard enough, the thought of having kids and raising them in this envi-ronment was a full-on slug to the noggin.* I contemplated this on the way home. I wondered where these people's kids were. Did they just stick them with nannies? Would Brigg and I have kids? What would Will's child look like? At the last thought, I became sick. Truly sick. I asked the driver to pull over, and I threw up just as Skipper had in the frat house foyer years ago, all over the side of the road. I couldn't believe myself. I hadn't even had a drink at the party! The driver got out immediately and brought me a bottle of water. I was grateful, and he drove slowly the rest of the way home, only commenting once, "Adjusting to altitude takes time, Ma'am. You'll come around." He was a sweet older fellow, and I knew he meant well, but I just nodded my head hoping to get home as fast as possible.

When we arrived, I went in the house, got more water, and made a peanut butter and jelly sandwich. It would have been better had there been chips to stick in the middle, I thought, and laughed a little remembering a certain beach day. I realized then and there that if I kept trying to block out all my memories with Will, then I'd be blocking out my entire childhood, and would have no childhood to reflect on. Besides, I already had so much negativity around me in this new place with constant worry that my fiancé wanted to make me a zombie and that I'd never feel at home. I needed to focus on happy memories, and not assumptions on what the rest of Will's life would become. I wasn't a part of it anymore, so it wasn't my business, anyway.

I took my snack out to the dock and sat on the end. It was chilly; even chillier than the New England coast on summer nights, so I was glad to have traded my heels for a blanket before I'd walked out. As I sat there eating and thinking, the sky above seemed a new type of clear. It was so starry that I felt like I was up in space with them right next to me. I could see the depth of the lights, and even the twinkling. It was something to smile about. A few bass from the stocked lake popped up to grab some bugs and made a little splashing sound… *like the snapping turtles.* This was going to be harder than I thought. Every single thing reminded me of him. I knew then and there I needed a hobby, or I was going to suffer. So instead of running from my pain, I just started… well… running.

Once I'd acclimated to the altitude, my daily walks had become jogs, and sometimes full-on runs with occasionally sprints. The summer passed and fall took on different colors and views. One morning, I had to take pause to admire an overlook next to the trail I'd been running on. Looking out over a valley from my mountain edge, I was able to see a contour of yellows and oranges and watch the quaking aspen around me; shivering in the wind while becoming naked as their little yellow leaves were blown away. All throughout autumn, I enjoyed the splendor of watching the season change. I watched the bucks start to come out of the woods looking for mates, the squirrels gathering food for the winter, and owls beginning to pack more into their nests for extra warmth. That warmth seemed to pass quickly though, and winter did not come with a slight flurry. Rather, it came with a blizzard. I suppose folks there would say it was just the start of the season, as most were looking forward to skiing anyway. But I was completely unsure how to approach this sort of weather. Brigg's family had been skiing in the area since Brigg was a little boy, so he knew how to drive, how to dress, and how to enjoy the winter sports. I knew none of it. I had never seen snow so deep and fluffy. To help me adjust, he thought it'd be best to send me out with the local ladies and suggested a day of shopping in the resort town's downtown area. I was quick to think *heck no*, but cabin fever forced me to cave, so I agreed to let them pick me up and go out for an adventure one day.

Candy came to pick me up in her SUV. She had a few cars, and it seemed one for each season. This car was her "snow car," as she noted. We arrived after parking on the side of the main street, which had miraculously been plowed flawlessly.

The other ladies met us inside a restaurant so we could grab lunch before shopping. It wasn't bad, and—with less alcohol and fancy accessories—they seemed to have better conversation. I believe I was the only one who had a burger for lunch, and I thought it funny when they all ordered dainty little salads. I believe they found it equally amusing when I finished my entire plate. Or perhaps they couldn't figure out how I stayed as trim as them, by eating such food. Perhaps they didn't realize running and hard work really *could* trump plastic surgery!

When lunch ended, we wandered around town. While they all wore furs, I wore an insulated barn coat. Perhaps Brigg had sent me with them so he could finally rid me of the coat after all! I didn't fit in, but they didn't seem to take notice. They were much too busy looking at jewelry. The other women continued ahead following the window trail of handmade gifts, designers, and gold (perhaps from prospectors past), but one particular window of a shop made me stop dead in my tracks. There on a wooden crate display behind a cold wintry window, was a pair of real, western cowboy boots.

Chapter 20:

ALMOST GONE

The women had come back looking for me, only to find me sitting void of expression in a café window drinking hot chocolate. Their kindness was unexpected, and they gathered to offer some compassion. I'd still not spoken even an ounce of what my issue was, but they made small talk about this and that, and I tried to listen intently; if not just to take my mind off [the unspoken] Will. They were accustomed to covering any issues they had with make-up and alcohol, and I tried to be sympathetic in my own way: realizing they just didn't know how to help me, even if they wanted to. My thoughts of Will had gotten to a point of no return, and ironically—at this point—that's all I wanted to do: return. Sitting in a café in a busy town and grey wintry world, surrounded by women who looked like snow bunnies, I just wanted to be home. Sadly, I didn't even know where home was anymore. I felt so lost.

They convinced me to shop a little more, and I treated myself to a complete winter running outfit. From head to toe, I was ready to face the elements, and run my gloom away.

The next morning, I would be back to avoiding the mindless banter of the neighborhood yuppies, and back to focusing on fresh air and getting lost in nature. It was my one peace of mind in this new world, and I wasn't about to let the weather stop me. Brigg gave me a kiss and headed out to work that morning, as usual. I had known he'd be busy after we'd moved, but his work often kept him out until the late hours of the night, and me with lots of time on my hands from sunup 'til sundown. I surely had to find ways to stay busy, and that I did. Running kept me healthy, and I often spoke on the phone with Narby and Skipper to keep my spirits up. Grocery shopping was an adventure of its own, as I constantly feared whacking the luxury cars with my shopping cart. I had grown to like cooking, though, so I found myself there often. Brigg had asked me a few times to host dinners for his partners and their wives when he realized I was good at it too. I learned that a few of those wives had been transplants like me—from humble beginnings. But unlike me, they'd given in to the lifestyle of the well-heeled. I knew in my heart I'd never succumb, and it was only a matter of time before I went insane. But how I would go mad, I didn't know. Would I just keel over and die from boredom and loneliness? Would I just up and leave one night and head back east? Would I purposely slide off one of the running trails and fall off a cliff for a fast death? I found it sad that my mind went there these days, but truth be told, I was depressed. Sadly, my physical health took a turn for the worst, too.

When out on a run one sunny afternoon in a freshly fallen snow that seemed to blind me as it reflected from below, I attempted to hop a log on my usual route. My feet slipped forward, and my back went behind me: snapping over the log. I felt a crack, and had it not been for Brigg who came looking for me later, I'd probably have frozen to death out there alone in the woods. The freezing to death part had not been in my thoughts of how I'd yield to the end of my time in the wintry western world, and so I was grateful to have been found. Maybe that was supposed to be my wake-up call that wishing for death wasn't the best idea after all.

Unfortunately, the accident had required spinal surgery, and being in a hospital brought me back to a bad place, and horrid memories. PTSD seemed to kick in, and flashbacks, nightmares, and hallucinations hit me hard. I'd not known I'd suppressed the feelings of my accident from high school for so long, and when they came to surface, they startled me beyond what I could handle. I was given a few pills for immediate anxiety relief, but when I was released from the hospital, I was put on painkillers as well. The heavy drug combination made my mental health completely crash, and I sunk to a very low place, very quickly.

One early evening, having finally found my footing and strength again, I made my way to the kitchen sink. Brigg wasn't home, as usual. The sun was setting, but I couldn't see it behind the gray clouds that had rolled in with another light snow. The light was fading from the sky, and even the outdoors—my normal place of inspiration—seemed discouraging. My insides felt like what I saw through the window: cold and miserable. My body and mind felt dead. I had taken with me to the kitchen my pain medication so I could wash down the usual pill with a glass of water as always. As I unscrewed the lid, and put a pill in my hand, I became distant for a moment as I looked down into the little container full of large white pills. As I put the lid back on and placed it next to the sink and got a glass from the cabinet, I stared out over a stark gray lawn in a world that had become foreign. The pond was as frozen as my heart, and it chilled me to the bone. I started to think there was nothing left to live for. I figured things could only get worse, and there was just no point to living. There was no hope in my future, and I had run too far from my past. I started to fill my water, but the phone ringing caused me to startle and drop the glass in the sink, and the pill on the floor. Luckily, neither broke.

I made it slowly to the side of the kitchen where the phone sat on a table, and I answered mechanically out of habit, "Hello?" I sounded dejected, and lifeless.

"Kate! What the heck? I've been calling for days and leaving messages!" Skipper was frantic and worried beyond belief.

"Oh. I didn't even know you called." I was telling the truth. Since I'd been home from the hospital, the phone had been turned on silent to allow me for better rest. I'd not even thought about checking messages either since my head was in such a haze. I wasn't myself, and Skipper could hear it in my voice immediately.

"Narby and I have been worried sick! Where is Brigg and why didn't he call us back to let us know you were okay? Or *not* okay?" she demanded. It was out of worry for me, but she sounded mad at him as well. Her words hit me hard too: *Where was Brigg?* She was right. How was work more important to him when I was home in bed trying to recover from physical and mental illness? I needed so much help, and he wasn't there to give me an ounce of it.

"Oh, now you're not going to speak?" Skipper went on, I think more so to see if I would react in my own feisty way so that it would reassure her I was okay. But I continued in a drained tone.

"Oh, I'm okay. Same old story out here as always: snow, gray... lonely." At that, I started to cry. *Lonely.* I really was. I cried for myself, I cried missing Narby, and Skipper, and the Pine Barrens. Most of all, I cried for Will. All those years, after I'd locked him out, I'd never had a chance to cry for him, and now I did. I had too much time on my hands, too much time to let the memories of him haunt me. I fell to the floor, and the back pain was searing. I couldn't get up, and I just laid there crying.

Skipper was a wreck herself now, knowing she wasn't there to help. "Stay put. I'm coming out there. I'm calling Brigg, and I'm flying to come see you." She stayed on the phone with me long enough that I could tell her I was okay and had gotten back to my feet. "Do. Not. Move. My dad will borrow his friend's jet, and I will be there ASAP." She made it very clear I had no say in the matter, and that was that.

We said our goodbyes and hung up.

I waddled slowly back to the sink to pick my glass back out, and filled it with cold water, placing it next to the sink. I bent slowly to pick up the pill. I stood there, once again with my pill and glass. The outside gray was almost too much to bear. I put the glass down so I could pick up the pill container again, take the lid back off, and put the lid down next to the sink. I stood there looking out into the flurries that now came down more heavily, my mind wandered to a memory of Will: *We were standing in a warm, sunny meadow, holding flower stems and blowing dandelion fuzz all over. They blew all around us, swirling in the air,* just like the snow falling. Tears rolled down my face, but I wasn't crying. I was still. I couldn't run anymore. I looked down into the bottle of pills and thought about dumping the entire bottle down my throat. In a split second, almost like something else had taken over my body, I dumped them down the drain instead, along with the one in my hand and turned on the spigot and disposal. I was not going to overdose. The memory of Will had just saved my life. *He* had just saved my life... again.

Skipper arrived less than ten hours after we spoke. Even a slight snowstorm couldn't keep her away, and she barged right in the house when she got there, and I had only wondered how she had gotten past the security guard at the neighborhood gate. When Skipper was mad, nothing could stop her. I was on a couch in the library, and Brigg was at the wet bar making himself a bourbon on the rocks. Skipper ran over to me and sat down, took my hands in hers as she looked as deep into my soul as she could, and hugged me in tears. As she made eye contact with Brigg when he entered the room, her eyes were red with anger and filled with rage, but she held back from scolding him. For the entire time she'd stay (and she planned on staying 'til winter was over and I was fully recovered), she would keep peace. She had so many things she wanted say to him. She knew him well—for as long as I had—and was horrified how he could have let me get to near death before he realized how poor of condition I was in. But like Will had done with me in the past, she would gently help me recover. It occurred to me at some point during Skipper's stay that I seemed to be destined for disaster: loss of parents, bullied at school, a car accident, losing Will, and now this awful recovery while being stuck in some cold, alien, fancy place. I knew I was a good soul, and I couldn't figure out why it seemed the universe was out to hurt me.

Once the holidays had passed (with Skipper and Narby present for all of them), and winter came to its peak, I had recovered. I insisted Skipper go home and resume her own life, but she stayed. I couldn't run again any time soon, but we worked out in my gym in one wing of the house, and she was my physical therapist and trainer all in one. Skipper had always had a killer body, and, by the time she was done with me, I think I was in the best shape of my life, too. She'd started me slowly, and with lots of stretching, of course. Seeing me become strong again, but the fact that she hadn't seen me become much happier, she suggested one last thing to make it through the rest of winter: a girl's trip to the Keys. She'd finally drag me along on one of her fancy tropical holidays, and this time, I didn't think twice.

"So, what do you think?" she asked, when we'd gone to lunch in town one day.

"In. One hundred percent I'm in," I replied.

She jumped up from the seat at one of the many cafe's in town, practically launching her chair into a passing waiter and scaring the bejesus out of some celebrities in town on winter holiday. "YES! I knew I'd crack you one day!"

The year before, I knew I was bound to crack at some point; I just didn't realize it'd be in the form of caving in to going on a tropical vacation with Skipper.

Chapter 21:

SOUTH

Key West in February is warm and inviting. The sun is out, the breeze is constant, and the people are happy. There are no weekend warriors; there is no "season." There is no snow; there are no pretensions. The place and the fun are daily, and nightly, and never-ending all year long. I'd never traveled much, mostly because I had always been content right where I was. But I wasn't going to lie: flying in over turquoise blue water, on a private jet, with little speckled islands here and there—and dotted with white sailboats—was pure ecstasy. Just like years ago when I'd invited Will to the prom and had a chance to see autumn from above, I now had a chance to see sailboats from the air, and not just the top of the lighthouse. It was a full-on aerial view of tropical seaside splendor.

On the tarmac, a driver was waiting. I couldn't believe it: it was the same man from years ago at college—Skippers butler! Though this time, he was dressed in a Hawaiian shirt and flip flops. He was on his own vacation, having come down from a more northern Key to pick us up. I was glad to see Skipper's family had such a big heart to send a hard-working man on his own, well-deserved vacation. I had known from day one that she was a good egg born from good people, and here was proof. After a big reunion hug for us both, he loaded up our things, and off we went to the resort. We'd have stayed at a family friend's waterfront house, as Skipper noted, but it was such short notice that they already had other friends visiting. In true Skipper fashion, the second-best choice was a penthouse at a beachfront resort at the southernmost part of the island. No sooner did we arrive at the place than her butler was off with our bags, and we were sitting on chaise lounges on a dock over the ocean with rum runners in our hands. I really hadn't become much of a drinker (even though being surrounded by so much booze over the years), but boy did that cocktail taste good!

"Remember the old days of big girl Shirley Temples?" she laughed, and I laughed with her, reminiscing. In fact, the rest of the day was just that: drinks, old memories, and laughter. By the time dinner rolled around, we were happily dizzy from our cocktails, and we wandered into town. Sun was setting, and we could hear the nightly celebration over at the pier. These people were my kind of people. They celebrated even the simple things like a sunset, like Will had. *Will*. I missed him so much it hurt.

Dinner was simple. A nice quaint place, yet full of history and lots of people, sat on the water's edge next to the marina. People were tossing food scraps into the water as they ate, and giant tarpon shoved each other out of the way for a bite. Tropical drinks flowed, live island-style music played, and everyone was happy. I did not expect such a place from Skipper, but for me it was perfect. And even she seemed at home. It was exactly what I needed to escape the forest of misery I'd left back out west. Snow was replaced with sun, loneliness replaced with plenty of smiling people, and I finally had time to catch up with an old friend, as my old self.

By the end of dinner, I'd had one too many drinks and Skipper stared at me sometimes, seemingly deep in thought, but also completely shocked in a funny sort of manner. For the first time, I'd had more to drink than she had. Whatever it was I was saying it had her in quiet amusement. We eventually flagged ourselves from the final rum drinks of the day and walked back to the resort. En route, with the sweet scent of jasmine and tropical vine-grown flowers in the air, we looked around and admired the old two-tiered decks of the historic mansions on the side streets. We tried to have an adult conversation, chatting about the architecture and décor, but all was cut short when a man driving a golf cart, along with his boyfriend, yelled out, "Check out the strip club! The men there really know how to shake their June bugs!" Skipper and I fell over on each other laughing hysterically, and she even went backward over a low fence into someone's soft hedge. It was like our old wild times, and it was so nice to reconnect. We laughed all the way back to our rooms, and sleep came fast from all the booze, walking, and sun earlier that day.

Come morning, Skipper had a little treat up her sleeve: sailing. I had never been on a boat this far south, and to be gliding over water so clear, filled with reefs, tropical fish, and dolphins within arm's reach, blew my mind. I couldn't stop smiling. Skipper noticed, and she was proud that what she'd brought me here for had been accomplished: I wasn't depressed anymore. The sun, salt, and sand had done the trick as always. Once our captain had slowed to anchor in a calm spot for lunch, Skipper's conversation took a more serious and curious approach.

"Kate, last night… umm…" She just stopped, smiled, and looked truly as if she didn't know how to continue with what she had to say.

"Skip? What's up?" I was curious myself now.

Still intrigued, and finding me cute for something I must have said or done, she just said it straight forward, "Who's Will?"

If it hadn't been for the trampoline in the center of the catamaran to hold me, I'd have fallen off the boat. *Will.* I hadn't heard, nor said, his name out loud for almost five years. *How did she know?*

As I sat there with my mouth gaping, she pried, "Well? Talk!"

I finally found my words, "How 'bout you tell me what you know first. And how you know it!"

"Girl, last night at dinner, you were beyond tipsy. You just started spilling about some guy named Will. I mean, it's one thing to get a little flushed in the cheeks from cocktails, but honey your face was all rosy and all smiles!"

Oh, my goodness. What had I said? Skipper went on to tell me exactly what it was I'd rambled on about, and luckily, it was more of silly childhood stories than my feelings. But as she watched my face when she repeated the prior night's heart pour, she saw in my eyes there was more to this "Will" than I had spoken about. She looked genuinely sad for me as I tried to hold back emotion. As I'd learned long ago, Skipper was a good listener when she wanted to be. And at that moment, I could see she'd never wanted to listen and help more. So, I told her. I told her everything.

Thank goodness she had chartered a private boat for us. The captain and crew were out of hearing range and Skipper and I sat with our legs curled below us on the trampoline, and continued nibbling on our lunch, while I told the story that I'd kept inside for half a decade. It seemed even longer than that to get it all out, but when I was finished, she knew the most important thing: I was in love with someone named Will. I had always been in love with Will, and my heart was broken not knowing where he was, how he was, what he was doing, and if he thought of me, too.

"Kate, you must really care about this guy to have kept your feelings about him private for so long. But you moved on. You are with Brigg. Isn't that what you want for the rest of your life?" I knew she was saying it more to bring to light what I really wanted, than believing I was ready to settle for someone who left me for dead when I was actually almost there.

It almost sounded like she was channeling Narby's voice as she said everything. It all hit me hard. The fact was, I didn't belong in my new life, but I'd separated myself so far from the old one, that I didn't know where I could pick up.

Skipper continued talking again when she noticed I was too deep in thought to speak.

"Whatever happens with Will, or anyone else for that matter, know that you have me. You will always have me. You're like a sister," she said and held my hand, and it gave me a sense of being okay. "Kate, listen, my heart has been broken time and time again. More so by women than men. So, for me to have found someone like you—so true blue—means the world to me. The one guy I ever truly cared about stopped talking to me because of another woman, in fact. So, for me to even trust another girl is huge. I don't just trust you, I love you. You are family. You are the friend I always wanted." She looked sad, and continued with her story, when she saw my empathy. "I had known another girl from an all-girls camp I went to in the summer. We boarded there together. Turned out, her family's home was not too far from my own, and we started riding our horses together so we could keep in touch in back home. I saw her at competitions, we rode on trails together sometimes, and I thought I had a close friend in her. She was a few years older, and I looked up to her like a sister. There was a guy from my childhood too, much like Will is from yours, and we had our own love story that came to an unexpected and sad end. I confided in her about everything, and how I was so hurt that he just stopped talking to me one day. I poured my heart out and told her I felt crazy reaching out to him time and time again trying to figure out what happened. Instead of helping me with my situation, she spread rumors about me around the barn, treated me like I was nuts, and she even made up stories to tell him and make me look crazy and mean-spirited. Of course, the worst of it: I lost the guy of my dreams." She looked so sad now herself, and I squeezed her hand to let her know I was there for her too. She sniffled a bit when I did this—trying to suck up the last of the tears and then tried to make light of the whole thing with a little giggle, saying, "I mean, I guess I should have known not to trust a girl who had a gossip column at her dad's equestrian magazine called 'The Barn Girl Blabs'!"

We both laughed heartily and remembered that we were better people than that girl who'd hurt her, than Kitty, and the sad women like

Candy back where I now lived. They all lacked something we didn't: a wholesome self-love. They were jealous, desperate for attention, and would probably never have loves like we had... or maybe *still* had. I only hoped the best for all of them, of course, since it wasn't my nature to hold a grudge, but I hurt then for both Skipper and me to have lost the loves of our lives as well. I was moved deeply to know Skipper did have more soul and wisdom than most had given her credit for. I realized then: we all hurt over different things in different ways. For this, I comforted her just the same. But for me, my love with Will was deeper than the water below us and spanned the surface of the entire sea. *I'd have done anything for that boy*, and when I said it out loud, I knew then and there that my leaving him had been a terrible mistake.

"It's true Skip, I would do anything for him. And even after all that's happened between us, I'd still walk to the ends of the earth for that boy."

It was strange to hear me say "boy," when the fact was, Will was a man now. *Would I even recognize him if I ever saw him again?*

That night after a whole day of sailing, we wandered the streets of Old Town and Skipper went into a cigar shop, first letting me know the owner knew her family and kept a stash of Cuban cigars in the back just for close friends. It never ceased to amaze me that Skipper and her family had friends in high places, and places all over the world! I stayed outside, and then wandered next door into another little shop. It had touristy trinkets and some local crafts as well. I picked up a silly little sailboat model and knew Narby would love it. I headed to register to check out, when something caught my nose. I turned slowly toward a little display of white flowers, on a table lined with beautiful little twinkling strands of lights. The whole set-up surrounded a tiny bottle of perfume: lily-of-the-valley. My heart stopped for a moment. The smell took me back through an entire decade with one sniff. I picked up the tester and rolled a bit behind my ear. The smell seemed to wrap around me like a hug, and I closed my eyes. I took one of the perfume bottles with me to the counter, along with the little boat, paid, and walked out.

I met back up with Skipper again outside the neighboring stores, and she started talking about the heavenly scent of cigars. She stopped suddenly though when she got a whiff of my perfume, and said, "Wow, that is completely your scent!"

I laughed, seeing she was back in true Skipper fashion, matching personality with material, and this time scent. It was just her thing, but I loved her for it all the same.

Once back to the hotel after the long day of sailing, a night of shopping, and another nice dinner, sleep came fast. I didn't bother to shower since I was so tired and had a good "sea bath" from jumping off the boat earlier anyway. *I did it when I was a kid. Who really cared if I missed one shower!*

When I shut my eyes, the last thing I smelled was the scent of sweet lilies from days past, and that night I dreamt about Will. The first time we met played over and over in my mind as I slept. Our entire timeline of memories danced around and around in my head, and I fell asleep with a smile. It wasn't over. *We* were not over.

Chapter 22:

EAST

Morning in Key West came with the smell of tropical flowers, tiny lapping waves, a warm breeze, and one thing on my mind: writing. Having forgotten how much I loved it, and since I couldn't run for the time being, I decided then and there to stop trying to escape my childhood, and – instead – embrace it. I realized I was so fortunate to have had such a wonderful childhood, from two different places no less, so it would be terrible of me to just throw it out. My life as I knew it at that moment, and who I'd become, was because of my past. The good and the bad; I was going to write about it all. I called Narby asking her to send me my journal as soon as she could. I knew in my heart she'd have not thrown it in a fire as I'd directed years ago, and she hadn't.

I met Skipper for one last breakfast in the warmth of the tropical winter, and I told her my plan. I was happily taken aback to see how supportive she was. She knew I wanted to forget the pain I was dealing with back home and focus on something positive. Not to mention, I'd finally said out loud to another, the story of Will and me or at least how much of it I could share in such a short period. But she got the point: I was in love with him. I was deeply, madly, insanely in love with Will. I figured the most that would (or could) come of it at that point, was a thank you note in the form of a novel to let him know I was grateful for our time spent. No matter how we'd left off, he needed to know I was appreciative for what had come before the devastating end. He wasn't a bad man after all; he had just gotten caught up in a bad situation. I still had no idea what he was thinking to have been with Kitty, but if I let the thoughts eat me alive, I wouldn't make it through the winter. Writing about the good times was going to help me get through, however. It would be a good thing, and I could sense it; Skipper could too. She had a push of support like never before. I was sure her encouragement was part anger toward Brigg and who he'd become, but – more so – her shear love for me as a friend and wanting to back me in anything I did. The return home would be a bright start: if even in the middle of [what could have been] the darkest winter of my life. Skipper was taking the jet home, and she sent me on my way with an optimistic smile on a commercial flight back west, as I insisted she let me do. She had spoiled me enough, so I'd politely declined a ride from her.

My flight back west had been smooth, and the ride from the airport back to the house was just the same. Brigg was nowhere to be found, as usual, upon arrival, but this time, I didn't feel alone. I had something all to myself again: my writing. Everything I'd loved had slipped away slowly over years and years. I didn't realize it, but I had sacrificed so much of myself and who I was, just to follow a man around. And worse: to follow a man just to escape another one! I wondered how I would grow in spirit and strength if just being someone evasive, spineless, and a follower. It wasn't me. It wasn't who I was my entire life, and I mustered up the strength to reflect, and remind myself that it was never too late for a fresh start. Perhaps life was full of fresh starts, and this was mine. My story was going to be a great love story: *my* love story. And I even set my mind to getting it published. I was going to become the writer I always wanted to be. I wasn't going to settle. I wasn't going to change who I was. I was going back to my dreams, and I was going to make the best of any life I'd end up in. Somehow, I knew being with Brigg and this new life wasn't going to be forever. Skipper had felt it too but wanted to give me the time and space to figure it out completely on my own. She had listened more than ever on that trip, and perhaps to let me listen to my own words, and let them truly sink in. I was unhappy, but I wasn't going to let it control me. I was going to find my own happiness again, and I would do it alone. Only this time, *alone* didn't sound like such a bad word. It sounded like something to be proud of. Arriving back home proved the first glimpse of hope, if even in a big, lonely, mansion of a house.

As soon as my journal had arrived, I got to work. I spent hours upon hours, writing out ten years' worth of memories, hoping in the end to share my story with the world. Surely it was a great expectation, but I'd never known someone to share a love like Will and I had, and I didn't want it to go to waste. Once I finished the book, even if not getting published, I figured the worst that could happen wouldn't be so bad after all. I could send it to a bookbinder, and have a few copies made: for me, for Narby, a few friends, and maybe even Will. I could open it when I wanted, and when feelings got too overwhelming, I could close the book and put it on the shelf for the time being. Whatever was to come of it, I knew it'd be positive. I was back to a place of enlightenment and hope, and I wasn't going to let a darn thing hold me back. But like all times when pushing forward, there are stumps in the trail. This time, my stump was a phone call.

On an evening similar in weather to the one when I was in the face of near death before I'd gone to the Keys, I sat at my writing desk: pouring out the story of my life. Winter had mostly passed, but the cold hadn't gotten to my bones this time around. Being alone, being the black sheep, and being mostly trapped inside didn't stop me from plugging ahead. When I answered the phone to Narby's solemn voice, coldness came over me though. I knew something was wrong, and I knew the book would have to go on hold for a while. The news caught me off guard, and really broke my heart. Farmer Russ had died.

After the hour-long phone call, I hung up and collected my thoughts. For the first time in almost five years, I had to go home.

The next morning, I woke up and started packing once again. It seemed like it'd been only yesterday I'd been unpacking from Key West. However, my focus on the book had gotten me through those following months of winter, and I hadn't even realized the snow was melting, and spring would be only around the corner. Back home, spring would have already hit in the different climate, and I could picture the bulbs starting to peek up around the farm. I was excited to return. The feeling inside me was the anticipation of when having first returned to the island: filled with memory, but also great loss. Only this time, it was ten times greater. I didn't know if it was my drive to reconnect with old faces, the place itself, or the thought I might even see Will (which I wasn't even sure I was ready to do), but something in me stirred. I was going back. My return was for a sad reason, but nonetheless… I was going back *home*.

When I was finished packing and while waiting for my ride, I found Brigg sleeping on the couch. I wasn't sure when he'd gotten in the night before, but I wandered over from the kitchen into the grand lodge-like family room and sat down on a big leather ottoman opposite his sleeping body.

"Hey. You okay?" I questioned him softly, touching his forearm.

"Hey…" He replied; sounding groggy and smelling like some sort of strong liquor. *Goodness, he really had turned into his father!* Over the years, I'd gotten to know his family well, of course. Although I had never approved of their drinking, I had always had a place and someone to escape to: Brigg. But since we'd moved, the stress of deadlines, meetings, and business dinners had caught him in a drinking pattern of his own. It had started as mild stress-relief I'd supposed, but it'd gotten to a point over this past winter, that it was daily, nightly, whatever. *Had I been a terrible and unthoughtful person myself to have overlooked my fiancé's need for help, while I selfishly wrote and stayed in my own little world?*

I waited for a bit for him to reply, but finally had to speak up when I realized he was just to bleary to finish.

"I have to fly home. Farmer Russ died," I said gravely.

The most unexpected reply came from Brigg's mouth, and I was horrified.

"Eh, he was old. It happens," he mumbled, starting to sit up.

"What?" I asked, immediately angered.

"Remember that guy down by the dock from back in college?" he asked, completely arrogant with his evasion of my own question.

"Yes," I said firmly, now furious but managing to keep my feelings inside.

"I heard he croaked a while back. Fell in the bay or something because he was drunk and drowned. At least your old farmer man probably had dignity," said Brigg.

I had no desire to humor him and reply. I was floored he could make fun of the man down on the docks I'd always thought he'd given respect and privacy to, floored he had the nerve to comment on Farmer Russ without any sympathy, and floored he'd not even asked if I was okay. Not even having ever met my farm family, he had no right to say anything about them. I was disgusted. I shook my head, and, as he got up to get himself coffee, he completely ignored my quiet emotions. With that, I grabbed my travel bags, and headed straight to the foyer to wait for the bell to ring. Luckily, I only had to wait a few minutes, and then I could be taken away; away from Brigg and his stifling, snobby sanctimoniousness. Brigg must have picked up on the fact that I was mad, but what he didn't know was that it was over between us. I was done. I didn't have time to end it then and there because I had to focus on my trip. Later would come soon enough and I'd break up with him with peace and class: both of which he'd never taken from me, nor would ever have in his own heart.

The trip home was more like a trip to the past. Though some trees had gotten bigger, and a few signs along roads had faded paint, nothing had changed. Unlike my trip back to the island so long ago, there was no hesitation with this venture. Not even the final memories of shutting down had blocked off my heart, and the moment I'd been driven back into town by way of the pines with Narby driving after she'd picked me up at the airport, I felt content. I felt at home.

Spring had come as I'd always remembered it: with bees, flowers, and muddy roads from thawing snow. It felt alive, and new, and ready for a new part of life to begin; just like me. I wasn't sure what I was even thinking by "moving forward," but at least being back home was a step in the right direction, if even being home for such a sad event.

There were no words to explain the gloominess of such a great loss floating through the air. People walked with their heads down, tractors lined the street in a long row—having come over from other farms in a show of great respect, and even the town hall's flag was at half-mast. Everyone was in mourning, and the entire town had gathered to remember such a great man. We all felt his warmth even if he was gone; through the breeze that flowed with the scent of the fields, through the sun that shown down on the dirt roads and through the tears that people shed remembering him. He would always be in our hearts.

Many people spoke at his funeral, and at some point it occurred to me Brigg had stayed home. I didn't know why this hadn't processed in my head earlier; after all, I'd been alone since I'd last spoken to him. Perhaps I had hope he'd have shown up a bit after me on a private company plane since I'd already been in town a day before the ceremony. But Brigg was nowhere. Not I, not a funeral for a truly wonderful human being, nor a show of respect for anyone would take him away from his beloved resort project. As I sat there listening to old friends speak in memory of Farmer Russ, I stiffened; trying to focus, but more to hide my anger at my fiancé.

Once outside of the church, a plane flew over as a salute to our late friend. I recognized the aircraft from the old airport nearby and thought it was kind they had come to pay their respects, as well, and even from the sky. It seemed the earth, the people, and even the blue above were sad to see Farmer Russ leave the earth. We all just imagined he'd stay by us forever—if only in spirit.

A celebration of his life followed at the local bar, which also served as a potluck buffet that day. Everyone brought a meal, and it turned into a commemorative party. Beer was on the house, people laughed, toasts were made, and it was just how he'd have wanted to be remembered. I caught up with old friends too. Dorey, Mrs. Mills, Mr. Leeds [minus the skunk], and Randy were beyond delighted to see me back home, and their hugs proved so. With each embrace, they seemed to hold me as tightly as possible: silently encouraging me never to leave again. Home was where my heart was, and I had no intention of returning west any-time soon; at least for now. I needed time home to regroup and recon-nect, and we all did until the sun set. No one mentioned Will, though, and he was nowhere to be seen.

I found my roots again back on the farm with Narby, of course. I had decided after the funeral that I'd just stay a week or so to catch up and help if she needed it. We caught up day after day, and she filled me in with all I'd missed for the time I'd be away at college, and for the past year living out west. But my telling her of my own year—and [especially] winter—had caught her attention most. In fact, she was left flabbergasted after I told her how Brigg had treated me as if I were invis-ible, and how I'd suffered through the cold months with my own mental health struggles of PTSD, depression, and more.

"Had it not been for Skipper taking me south to some warm sun, I don't think I'd have made it, Narby." I spoke, very sure of myself, but at least calm enough to finally talk about it openly.

She felt awful. "I wish I'd known, Kate. Gosh! I wish I'd been there for you," she said as she held my hands and her eyes welled with tears.

"Narby, it's not your fault. Any pain in my life has never been your fault. Don't you even think for a second it was! What was happening with Brigg was something I brushed under the rug, and it was my own fault that I suffered because I never spoke up." I assured her it would all

193

be alright, but she missed the *"was"* part of my relationship with Brigg. Soon enough I would let her and Skipper know it was over.

We held hands, and I told her everything. After I'd finished story after story, and example after example of how lost I'd become out there, she felt it was time she filled me in on everything I'd missed back home as well. She started off lightly though, as she knew I was reeling from all I'd just come from, and wanted to ease me into the info she was about to pour; info that she'd wanted to tell me for years, but had never found the right time.

"That ceremony for Farmer Russ was so nice," she said. It was small talk though. I could feel it.

"It was," I said, graciously blunt, hoping to encourage her to get to the real matter that I could tell she was holding back.

She continued though. "It was nice for the plane to have flown over. Shame the old pilot who had owned it wasn't here to actually fly over himself."

"What?" I was perplexed and asked. "He died, too?" *Gosh, what else had I missed?*

"Yes. Right after you left to head west, he passed," Narby spoke. "I know moving had been hard on you, and I didn't want to put more on your plate by telling you."

I understood, but still, I had another question: "If that wasn't him, then who was flying that plane?"

Her face said it all. She had no reason to voice expression because she wanted me to find my own. *Will.* He had flown over me just hours ago. We were both back in the same place—back in our hometown. My stomach turned a bit at this news. I wanted to see him, I wanted to hear from him what I'd missed, I wanted to hear him say he was sorry, I wanted to say I was sorry, I wanted to say congratulations for having gotten his pilot's license. *He could fly. He had become a pilot, and I had missed it all for my darn pride and running away.*

"Kate, after I returned from dropping you off at college, he came here to the farm. He was completely distraught, and, of course, I didn't have the heart to turn him away. We spoke one night, all night, and his eyes were like an empty blue sea. He was lost without you, Kate. The worst for him came two months after school had started again."

"How so?" I asked, having more anticipation with wanting to know everything at once.

"Kitty," she said, her face red with anger.

My god, what more could that monster have possibly done?

"Kate, the pregnancy was a lie," Narby said and she seemed to hold her breath for my reaction.

"Oh. My. God," I said. I felt sick, I felt like passing out, and I felt violent. I'd never felt such a rush of wanting to strangle someone. She must have heard it in my voice too. So, *this* is what Narby had wanted to tell me the night Brigg had proposed. I wanted to kill Kitty then.

In a rush of pain, anger, regret, and a million other negative emotions searing through veins, I stood up and ran outside. I ran, and I just started running. Narby ran after to follow me, but once she saw I was gone, she let me go, knowing I'd eventually find my way back.

Luckily, I'd put on sneakers that morning, and had been given clearance to jog lightly again by my back surgeon before I'd left, but I was running. I was sprinting. Full force like a plow through the woods, I was sweating out so much pent up hurt from Brigg and everything I'd suppressed. I cried then. I ran crying; crying for the hurt that Will must have suffered alone, without me by his side. I made it to the waterhole, and I hunched over on my knees: out of breath and crying out loud with agony. If anyone had been around, they'd have thought someone was being killed. "No! No!" I heaved out, over and over. My poor Will. My poor Will I'd abandoned.

Narby had been right in her mind that I would eventually return. I did, and she had set the table for dinner. She could see my eyes had been red from crying, and that I needed a shower, looking like a horse after splashing through puddles without care. I was covered from the knees down in mud, but my entire body was covered in shame. I had run from my best friend when he needed me most. *He must hate me,* I thought.

Dinner started quietly, and eventually Narby eased back into conversation. My shower had loosened my tenseness, and I was able to control my emotions again.

"He wanted to tell you, but you were already a few months into college, and he wanted you to focus on getting the journalism degree you always wanted. It killed him not to reach out. He eventually found out you were engaged because of the announcement in the paper, and…"

I cut her off, "Announcement? What Announcement?"

"Kate? Your little note in the paper?" she said, now looking completely lost.

"I didn't put anything in the paper. Narby, tell me what it said."

She spoke, still confused, "A week after Brigg proposed to you, an announcement appeared in our paper. I thought you wrote it."

I was horrified and thought out loud "Brigg. He wanted to control me; control everything! He even got into my hometown paper to take control? This can't be happening." My head was spinning again, and Narby watched as I tried to talk myself through the confusion.

Narby poured me a glass of red wine and told me to relax and just breathe. My anger from earlier with Kitty had returned. I didn't drink the wine though. If I would have picked up the glass, I'd have thrown it across the room. I was raging inside.

"Narby, does Will still live here?" I asked intensely.

She then poured herself a glass of wine and took a long sip. She sat back in her chair, almost defeated, and spoke again, "Once he read that article, he packed up almost as quickly as you had for college and moved."

"Moved where?" I shot my questions at her in rapid fire.

"South," she said but seemed to have little more to say. "To the Carolina's, I think."

I knew she had more detail, but she was not about to give it to me, worried I'd hop in the truck and speed off, and get into another accident. I clearly had a way of running from things, but this time, she was going to remind me that I had changed, and I did not need to run anymore. But I was determined to get as much as I could from her.

"And that was it? Did you ever hear from him again?" I kept prying.

"Nope. I heard from his dad though. He left to join Will in a new business down there within the year, and they've been there for almost five years now. Will got his license, of course, and they started a spraying company. He bought the plane you saw him in."

He'd done it. He'd followed his heart. He was a pilot after all, and she had just confirmed it. I smiled remembering this, and knew it was time to be happy for Will, stop running, and relax. I knew it was time to tell Narby that no one else would be leaving her. In fact, it was I who would be leaving Brigg and coming back home to the Pines: for good. But I was still curious.

"Where did he go after the funeral?"

"He flew the plane right back South again," she replied. "Randy told me."

A week later, I flew to my own house back out West.

Once I arrived, I approached Brigg as he headed out for some resort-related business, as usual. He seemed to have little time for me these days, and this day appeared no different. In fact, he seemed even more impatient than usual.

"What?" he snapped.

"I need to talk to you," I said. I was calm and collected.

"Can't it wait? I'm late for this meeting," he said. He was calmer now, but still letting me know business was first. "If you want to talk about your trip home to visit the rednecks, how about we grab dinner tonight in town?"

The redness I'd seen in Narby's face just a few days earlier when she spoke about Kitty, now showed on my own. I calmed myself enough to make my words very clear, and very loud. "No. I'm not a redneck, Brigg. I'm a Piney, from my head to my hiney, and I'm DAMN proud of it."

He laughed and walked out, slamming the door behind him. Little did he know that I'd be having the last laugh!

Throughout the day, I packed up the few things that meant anything to me and boxed them up. I called the driver we often used as a limo service and asked him to take my things to the shipping company we often used for bulkier packages, and then drive me to the resort. Brigg's car was parked in his reserved spot.

Regardless that he was now in the middle of a meeting, I barged into it, and walked right up to him. The other men looked astonished, but stood when I entered, to be respectful to a lady.

Everyone stayed silent, until I was a foot from Brigg's face, and stared him directly in his eyes.

"No." I said, my face as still as ice.

"What? Kate, I'm in the middle of a meeting here," he said and shifted on his feet a bit, uncomfortable and worried.

"My answer is no."

His voice quieted even more, "Can we talk about whatever this is in the hallway?"

"You've silenced me enough," I continued, now completely ignoring his request and need to avoid humiliation. "When you asked me to marry you, you never waited for me to reply. You stuck a ring on my finger and continued to rant and rave about this. All this." I spun around with my arms, seeming to finally take it all in; all I'd been pushed aside for. "So, my answer to you is no. I will not marry you." I slammed the ring down on his conference table, and only hoped it left a nice dent in the rare wood.

I walked calmly and collectedly back out to the car and rode all the way to the airport with the windows down. I breathed deeply, and once I settled, the only feeling that remained, was the East calling me back home.

Chapter 23:

HOME IS WHERE THE PINES ARE

Moving back home was quite possibly the easiest and most natural-feeling thing I'd ever done in my life. There was no force to run from a tragedy, no push to run from pain, no moving on someone else's terms. I was moving home for me, and to truly start my own life for once, in the place I chose. Narby and the hometown crew were happy to see me return, of course. It seemed like even the land welcomed me back, and it was good to know home was truly where the heart belonged.

Naturally, I decided to stay on the farm until I could find my own place. Narby had insisted, and deep down I think she hoped I'd just move in and stay permanently anyway! Any solidity in my staying would be determined by time and finance, of course. Since having graduated school, I never did have a chance to get a job, so I figured I'd just pick up where I left off at the paper. Although a temporary editor had been hired when the head of the paper had found out I'd moved west, the owner discretely let Narby know the job would still be available when I was ready to come back; and somehow they knew I would be. I told him I'd think on it. He knew, just like everyone else in town, that I'd been through a heck of a life and I needed a little time to settle back into it, to truly start fresh again. Starting over gave me great optimism, and I was covered in dirt and good hard work in no time. I promised Narby to help keep the farm as it was when we'd fixed it up years ago, and never let it go back into an abandoned slumber. The weeds and vines had seemed to grow a little extra, as if knowing I was coming home to give me a good project. The work would keep me busy but also give me time to clear my mind, and allow me to truly think through what I wanted for the future. I did think about Will and if he'd ever reach out but gave him the space he'd given me to figure things out on his own. I continued plowing through the writing of my book until the very last page. Once the sun had gone down each day after working around the property, I'd kept at writing diligently, and once my query letters had been sent to literary agencies, I knew I'd have to be patient for replies… if I'd ever even get one at all. Deep down, I knew someone would reach out. After all, this was the greatest love story I could possibly have written. At the least, I'd done just that: written it. I would always have my memories of the place I truly grew up, and the person who grew up alongside me.

Once spring had passed, the flowers had popped up just as I'd remembered them, but in larger groups. The property was splashed with palates of rainbow colors; the birds and bugs buzzed through the fresh air soaked with the essence of nectar and sweetness. I wondered if those creatures that flew around me were relatives of the creatures I'd once left, coming out and flying around just to welcome me home.

Another month or so past, and I had melancholy almost given up hope that my book would be considered. However, when out trimming a few rose hedges that had taken over the arbor out front near the gate, Narby came running out onto the porch with excitement and a face full of anticipation. She had a phone in her hand, and quickly shook her head with a smile, to encourage me to hustle to her and take the phone.

"Hello?" I'd answered, becoming just as excitedly anxious as Narby. She had gone back inside to give me privacy.

"Hello there!" the friendly agent continued to speak, saying my full name, and I could sense this was business, and something new was about to happen. "I'd like to request your full manuscript, and please let me know if you have any other agents reach out for representation."

We made some nice small talk as well, and although all advice I'd read as per choosing an agent suggested that I wait to speak to many before settling on one, this person got me. We were a perfect match, and I knew then and there I had a lifelong friend, and someone to represent me forever.

When I hung up the phone, I squealed a big "yay" of delight, and Narby hurried back out. I had a feeling she'd secretly been listening in the closest room to the porch.

She didn't waste time to get news, and asked, "Yeah?"

"Yes! Yes! Yes!" I was jumping up and down, for all the heart and soul—time and effort—I'd put into my book was now being recognized. "They didn't take me on yet, but I know they're going to love the book. I have a good feeling about this group Narby!" I squealed in joy.

A week later, once the agent had read over the full manuscript, we chose to work with each other after all. Of course, now the wait for which publishing company would pick me up would be an even bigger try of patience. At least the start of it had been put into motion. Who knew a small-town girl would have come full circle to write about her own childhood, enough to catch the eye of one of the most well-known, and bold agents in the industry?

It wasn't long before my agent called me back. We'd done it; my book deal with one of the largest publishing houses in the country was complete, and my advance was more than I could have wished for. Though it had never been my goal to make much money, it felt darn good to know it was *my* money, all earned *myself*. It wasn't Brigg's; it wasn't a free ride to live on someone else's terms and turf. I had done it, and I had done it all on my own.

Though Narby had some news of her own to share, she let days of celebration pass and my joy to settle to a level of normalcy once again, before sharing it.

"Kate, I'd like you to know something," she said, and I couldn't quite read her. If she were about to let on some bad news, I wouldn't be surprised. It had always happened that my cheeriest times were succeeded with downing info. I held my breath.

"The bait shop went for sale again a month ago," she spoke.

At least the news wasn't traumatizing, but still I wondered why she was sharing it with such an odd approach.

"I bought it," she said. I was floored; she seemed excited, but I could see she was holding something back, too.

"Narby. That's great! Right?" I reacted with excitement and confusion all at the same time, but she could also tell I was wondering what was going to happen with the farm.

So, she continued, "I'm going back. My heart is by the sea. It always has been. But I'm leaving you the farm."

My jaw dropped. I remembered when she'd given me the truck, but now she was leaving me her home?

"Narby, you can't… I mean…" I fumbled but I was in awe.

"Kate, you helped bring this place back to life, and I never want to see it die. Besides, this is where you belong. I knew it all along, and I want you to enjoy every second of being here, and all the joy it will bring you in the future." She didn't stop quite yet. "You know, I'm proud of you. You've been through nightmares in life and look what's come of it all. You're an author! You're resilient, you're intelligent, and something good is in the air. I can smell it."

It was funny to hear her talk to me like I was still a kid; like Will had always spoken to me like I was the younger one. *Will.*

I needed to thank her, so I spoke, "None of this would have ever happened without you, ya know. This place, my life, none of it, Narby. You took me in. You brought me to this magic town, and because of you I had the best childhood I could have ever asked for."

To avoid sniffling, and remain as steadfast as she'd always been, she kept on with her own explanation. "I want you to save your book money for whatever your future will throw your way. Don't even think for a second of buying this place from me because I already know you're considering trying to offer something." She was right; I was only seconds away from offering her my entire advance!

"Hey," she said one more time. "The farm comes with a truck, too."

"No. It's too much," I insisted, as she handed me yet another set of keys.

"I've never been much for new things," she said, commenting on her more recent purchase. "Besides, *Piney Power* needs to get out more. I can hear her calling my name in my dreams." She laughed at her own comment.

"Okay, Okay. But what about winter?" I kept trying to make sure she'd be okay and wasn't being manic with her giving.

"Are you saying I'm too old for cold?" she said, shutting me down, with a hint of pride and joke.

Chapter 24:

REFLECTION

Once Narby moved out for good, I was left alone with my own thoughts, a bit of silence, and boxes full of memories I needed to sort through, which had been stored throughout the property. Early in the season, on a beautiful summer day that wasn't too hot, I figured I'd start rummaging through one of the old barns before the season picked up and became to stifling to work outside much. Chipmunks scurried as I opened the big sliding doors, and I noticed the old blue truck was gone. *She'd sold it after all.* No wonder she'd finally parted with it. In the condition it was in, it would've never been repairable. What's more, seeing it must have brought her to her own bad memories, and thinking of the time she almost lost me. But my own memories swirled around me then. A breeze blew in with the scent of lily-of-the-valley, the chipmunks played hide and seek with me around the barn corners, and a few bits of straw from corn crates blew in the breeze. We'd packed breakables in them long ago (or at least what seemed long when I was a child), as per Will's resourceful suggestion. I wondered about him now. It was the first time I was truly alone with my thoughts of him in a positive light. I wasn't telling Skipper. I wasn't crying in a kitchen alone out west. I wasn't running away to school to escape him. I was home: just me, the elements of summer, and a book all about our childhood, about to be published.

I sorted through crates, boxes, and chests for hours, only stopping for sweet tea breaks on the porch back at the house. Come day's end, I'd finished going through the outside bins, and after making myself some dinner I still had energy I couldn't seem to tame, so I headed to the attic back in the house. As the house was so old, electricity had never found its way to the top floor, so I took up an electric lantern. The last thing I wanted to do in my [*my!*] new home, was burn it down with a real kerosene lamp! I found an old rocking chair, which was surprisingly dust-free, as was the rest of the attic. Narby must have gotten up there, on a lonely day, and went to work, cleaning. It hit me then how lonely she must have been with me being gone. It showed in many ways, especially how well the house had been kept. I put the little lantern on the top of a wooden ship's wheel table, one of the many nautical antiques that had been passed to Narby along with her farm. I started rummaging gently through the first boxes in arms reach. Upon opening a little cedar chest, I found old photographs from the island. Dating back to Narby's childhood, I was seeing images of the island from long before most of the scrubs pines and dunes had been taken over by lumber and boardwalk paths. Even the lighthouse once had a light-keepers' quarters and I was amazed looking at the images. The next box was more recent and made my heart stop: my first bits of childhood with my parents. I smiled as I flipped through the images. Memory after memory brought smiles and a few tears. The last box held what I had anticipated most since having realized these boxes were filled with photos: my childhood in the Pines. Picture after picture, Will and I gleamed with joy and adventure, dirty jeans, and wild hair. I could do nothing but smile then. But my smile faded slowly, and I became still as any deer I'd ever seen freeze in the woods when I picked up the last photo in the box. There in my hand was the picture of me and Will from prom. It was instantaneous how the tears came now. I held the picture to my heart, and sat back in the rocking chair, almost flipping it. I cried, and I cried, with no sound, just intense sniffing after each time I breathed out. I'd never cried so much for another human in my life. The sun had long set, and the attic darker than when I'd first walked up. When I finally settled from crying, and after a long while staring at the picture, remembering what it felt like to be held by him, looked at by him, and how his eyes were filled with so much love for me, I took the lantern and headed back downstairs with it. My room had been left as it was when I left for college, and I'd chosen that one to stay in when I'd moved back in. Just like the attic, the room had been cleaned pristinely, and I opened the window as always for fresh air: partly to feel the past on my skin, and partly to keep from soaring into longing for Will. I stared at the picture until my eyes closed, and I fell asleep that night with a head and heart full of the past, the present, and hopes of whatever would come.

Chapter 25:

Sugar Sand Road

Settling in for good was bittersweet. Coming back and forth from the grocery store or hardware store, I finally saw a for-sale sign go up at Farmer Russ's place, and it hit me hard. It was a sad time, but I tried to look at it as positive change. *Everyone is getting a fresh start*, I thought.

With that change, came the first changes in my own life, and my world as a novelist began. In fact, my first book signing was coming up; and it was only natural that it'd be home: at the Bogberry Festival. It was a place for locals, and even people from afar, to come and partake in what life was like in our neck of the woods.

My booth was set up across from the berry slide where kids of all ages [adults included!] slid through piles of unwanted berries that were too ripe to use for anything else. The result: people who looked purple, wet, and filled with laughter. It brought a smile to my face and day-long entertainment between my readers. Narby was the first in my line, of course: buying two copies of my book—one for her, and one for "good luck." She'd always been one with superstition, so I laughed at her silliness, as I always had. Other familiar faces were in line right behind her: Dorey, Mrs. Mills, the elders from the farm, and even Randy. Mr. Leeds had never been one to read, but he was present: dancing to the local string band with his skunk. I was shocked the little furry fellow was even alive. From what Mr. Leeds had told us long ago, that skunk had already been ancient. I wondered how many lives skunks had! I also believed it must have had an ear for music, as it seemed to enjoy being bopped around in Mr. Leeds' arms to the sound of banjos and fiddles. I smiled at the sight of it all; everyone did.

When the end of the day came and I'd made my farewells to everyone who'd come out to support me, Narby let me know she was stopping by the farm to grab some things before heading back to the island. She asked if I wanted to come along, but I politely declined. She hitched a ride with a friend from the island who'd driven her to the festival in the first place, and off they went. As for me, I wanted to take some time to myself to reflect and smile about all I'd accomplished. Since having been home, I'd not seen the town much again, as I'd been so involved in cleaning up around the property and digging through old treasures. So, I took this time to adventure.

I drove around to the outermost parts of town, and even the heart of places I once avoided. I returned to the site of the bonfire, and where I'd almost lost my life. No emotion struck my face as I looked down on that place, but – more so – a gratefulness for being alive and having good people there to have saved me. After hours of wandering, I decided the waterhole would be a good place to end my day. It would be nice to let my feet drift in the water, like the easy thoughts drifted in my head of what my future would bring.

I had never gotten used to seeing the for-sale sign at Farmer Russ's place, and eventually I was uneasy that I couldn't shake the sadness it brought me each time I saw it. For the time being, I needed to bury those feelings, and just reflect on the great day behind me, and the peaceful night ahead. When I arrived back at the house to park and grab a drink before heading out on a hike before it got dark, I noticed Narby had already come and gone. She had left a beautiful bouquet of flowers for me on the kitchen table, with a note of congratulations. I smiled and headed out. I sat for a while by the water, taking note of the beaver dam that remained and must have housed many generations of those buck-teeth babies over the years. The trees were the same, and what caught my eye most: the little patch of cranberries. It had spread over time, but, like the first time I'd seen it, one little red berry stood out. I couldn't believe it. Maybe it was good luck, and I had to laugh and smile. I lay back on the dock, which had become a little worn, but still held me with its strong planks as I left my toes to dip. I closed my eyes and listened to the pines blow in the wind, intertwined with the smell of the sweet pepperbush. I smiled with my eyes closed. Will wasn't there to watch me, but the forest was. I was home, and the saltwater in my veins was replaced then by copper streams, tall pines, and sugar sand. My heart was in this place, and I would never run from it again.

Once the sun started to set, I didn't stick around to watch the "sun stars" [as we'd named them years ago], twinkle through the needles. Since childhood, the paths we'd forged had become overgrown in places here and there, and I didn't want to get lost on my way back.

Once almost to the porch, I looked down the road in the final lights of day, back toward the farm I played on with Will as a child. I decided to keep walking. Perhaps I needed to say my own goodbye to the place, before it sold for good, and a next chapter would begin again. I wanted to pay my respects to the farm. It was the right thing to do.

However, when arriving, it seemed I was too late. I was shocked to see the sign was missing. *The farm had sold!* My heart became heavy, and I almost felt as if I'd never had a chance to say goodbye. Yet, there was something else I noticed: the end of the driveway was dusty, as if someone had just driven on it. I kept walking to turn the corner to see if maybe I could pick the brain of whoever had just arrived.

As I turned the corner at the dirt driveway, I looked up and shielded my eyes from the sun, which had almost set over the fields. Squinting, I could make out a truck. When I looked closer, I realized I recognized it: blue, with wooden planks above the bed. I couldn't believe it. Narby had fixed up the truck after all and bought the farm! That stinker! Now I knew why she said she was stopping back at the farm! Always with a surprise up her sleeve. I shook my head, smiling, walking toward the truck to give her a hug and laugh. But any humor, and joke, was cut short.

From the driver's side I could only make out the figure of a man with the sun behind him. He had on a farm t-shirt, jeans, and a pair of cowboy boots. What caught my attention the most were his blue eyes above a scruffy, short beard, which sparkled from the sun rays that came in behind him, enlightening the rough edges of his face.

He took the first steps toward me, and then he smiled: the same beaming smile, the same kind soul, the same boy from the sugar sand road years ago. It was Will.

My heart was truly in my throat, and I couldn't find a word to say. I could only move toward him. I came within a foot of his face, and we just stared at each other. My lips were apart, and my face must have looked dazed, but he didn't seem to notice, nor care what expression I wore. His face said enough. I was home, he was home, we were both home. I just had no idea what it all meant, what was happening, or what to say—let alone if I could even speak. Instead, he spoke.

His voice was different: older, deeper, yet still with the same joy and comfort of being in his own skin. "First..." He paused for a moment, as if to let me absorb the new voice that came from his lips, "... I'd like you to sign this, Katie." He pulled out a book from his back-jean pocket. *Narby was here! She'd given him the other copy of my book!* I watched his strong forearms as he brought it to his waist. I noticed he wore the belt buckle I'd given, and I watched his hands gently hold the book I'd written—the book I'd written about us. There was no way he'd had time to read it, but it didn't matter. He knew what the book was about. It was written all over his face.

I don't know how I even managed to speak at that point, but I found the strength for at least one, dry, and raspy word, "First?"

He continued, still unwavering with his beautiful smile, the most handsome smile, the most handsome man, I'd ever seen in my life. "Then, I need you to help me hang this sign on my new property here." It read: *Sugar Sand Farm.*